devil you know

aly welch

DUSKBOUND
BOOKS

ISBN: 978-1-968625-04-7

First Edition: November 2025

DuskboundBooks.com

Copy Edit: Cari Dubiel

Cover Design: Kaytalin McCarry

Formatting: G.A. Finocchiaro

For my parents

chapter one

Tiffany sat on stage in a dark club, a more intimate venue than the stadiums she usually performed in. No musicians. No dancers. Just her with an acoustic guitar, sitting on a stool. She wore a modest slip and simple black high heels, her wavy brown hair falling to her shoulders.

As she strummed the opening to "Stranger to Myself," Tiffany sensed an unhappy stirring in the audience. Against her better judgment, Tiffany peered into the crowd. The men and women began to shimmer and blur, like a shifting mirage. Their bodies shrank even as their fingernails grew into dagger-like claws, and their skin became green and mottled.

Tiffany rose from the stool, her eyes widening in terror. Her guitar clattered to the floor, forgotten. The men and women...no, the *reavers*—otherworldly monsters that could bend the very fabric of reality—surged toward the stage, hissing and growling and snarling Tiffany's name. She turned to run, but one of her ankles buckled underneath her. Tiffany fell.

A clawed hand grabbed her other ankle as Tiffany tried to crawl away. She saw stairs up ahead. If she could only reach them. Tiffany kicked the hands away, crawling closer to the base of the stairs. Was that smoke she smelled?

A door at the top of the stairs opened. A cruel, twisted face leered at her.

"Oh, Tiffany," Brendan said sadly. "How can you save the world if you can't even save yourself?"

"But how..." A burst of coughing stopped Tiffany from finishing her sentence.

The smell of smoke intensified.

"Fire!"

Tiffany sat up in bed and looked around the darkened room in a panic.

"No fire," said a gruff but soothing voice. "Only me."

Instead of smoke or flames, Tiffany saw Randy's concerned face as her eyes adjusted to the darkness. She heard a heavy thud as one of her cats, a gray tabby with a stub of a tail named Groucho Manx, jumped to the floor. Tiffany wrinkled her nose.

"Apologies for the smell. Morgan asked me to accompany her entourage to a late-night meeting on the old Vegas strip," Randy explained as he unbuttoned his white collared shirt to reveal a lean but muscular torso. "Some backroom in a sketchy casino. I'm not exactly sure how dealing with the local mafia figures into Morgan's plans, but it may be the cost of doing business in Vegas."

"Mafia?" Tiffany's eyes widened. "I thought the government made Sin City a little less sinful years ago."

"The players may have changed," Randy said, running a hand through his already mussed auburn hair. "The game remains the same. But for all her experience dealing with dangerous men, I'm worried Morgan has gotten in over her head this time. She seems..." His amber eyes narrowed in contemplation.

"Seems what?"

Randy looked at Tiffany. "It's probably nothing," he said with a shrug. "Do you know we never even talked about...well, you know. Not that I was expecting a big apology or anything. After all, she made the right call based on intel. It's the intel that was bad. But it's still weird acting like nothing happened at all."

"Maybe she thought things would be easier that way," Tiffany said.

"Maybe."

Tiffany watched with appreciation as Randy continued to disrobe on his way to the shower in their penthouse suite. Her smile faded as her nightmare came back to her. Though more than a year had passed since Morgan le Fay's nephew in disguise had held Tiffany captive in her Hollywood Hills home, he still haunted her dreams.

Brendan, like Tiffany, was half Fae. His mother, Vivienne, was one of three sisters who ruled over a dying kingdom in another world. Unlike Morgan, Vivienne had no love for this world, but nobody knew where Vivienne was or what she was planning, only that she certainly had a grudge to settle after Brendan's death.

Tiffany wasn't even clear on Morgan's plans. She just knew they included Tiffany and her influence as a pop star to…to do what exactly?

Save mankind from itself?

Or from an ever-growing number of malevolent beings from other worlds?

Tiffany sighed, snuggling into the silky sheets of her king-size bed. She was no closer to uncovering any latent Fae powers than she was when she first found out the truth about her origin. Her mother had been human, but her father, "John," was one of the Fae. Morgan had imprisoned him because she had forbidden the Fae from taking or creating life on Earth.

That was where John met Randy, a former ally of the Fae wrongfully accused of killing humans in his wolf form. Two years ago, Tiffany didn't even know shapeshifters existed. Now she was dating one. Randy helped John find Tiffany after someone released them and five other convicts for unknown reasons. Her father died confronting a pyromancer who worked for Brendan, but Randy's shapeshifter strength helped him survive the fiery assault. Tiffany hired him, in part to learn more about her father. But Tiffany had difficulty maintaining professional boundaries in close proximity, or at least that's what her therapist said. So now Randy was her boyfriend, and Morgan hired other Fae security to protect Tiffany.

After a whirlwind world tour in countries friendly to the Fae and a successful acoustic album release, Tiffany moved into an executive suite atop Avalon, a luxury resort owned by Morgan's Lafayette Corporation for a long-term residency showcasing her biggest hits. The nearby Excalibur Hotel and Casino hadn't been happy about the resort's name and theming, but settled with the Lafayette Corporation out of court. Morgan also promised Tiffany an opportunity to perform more intimate acoustic shows for her VIP guests—no doubt world leaders and businesspeople aligned with Morgan's goals.

Tiffany heard the shower trickle to a stop. She rolled over and pretended to be asleep. The bathroom door opened and closed. Tiffany was impressed by Randy's stealth as he crossed the room without a sound, but the mattress sank beneath his weight as he settled beside her. She giggled when he nuzzled her neck, his body longer smelling of cigarette smoke, only lavender vanilla soap and shampoo.

"Still awake, then?" His lips brushed against her skin as he spoke.

"I have to be up in a few hours for rehearsal," Tiffany said. "The show opens in less than a month."

"Okay," Randy said. He nipped at her neck, then rolled onto his back.

"So, I need you to help me go back to sleep." Tiffany sat up to glare at him.

Randy laughed and pulled her to him.

chapter two

"I'm not sure how I feel about this position."

"I think you're doing it wrong."

"Are you sure?"

Caitlyn Smith looked at Amber Mills, a dancer hanging precariously from a metal hoop covered in green fabric and suspended several feet above the stage of Avalon's Otherworld Theater. The presently upside-down woman wore her blond hair in a long braid that almost reached the floor. "Are you trying to do the transition from Man in the Moon to Lion in the Tree? If you untangle yourself, I can walk you through it from the beginning of the routine."

Amber pulled herself up until she was sitting on the lyra, holding the sides. She slid back to hang by her knees, still gripping the sides as she pulled out one leg, then the other to drop down to the safety mat. "I need a break." She sat down and reached for a water bottle.

"Not too late to trade apparatuses," Jade Ortiz Rivera said from across the stage. She sat massaging her feet while Emi Hamada rose higher and higher above the stage, wrapping pale pink silks around her legs and body until she was ready to perform an intricate drop.

The four women had been performing with Tiffany Sharp for a couple years in videos and on tour. Now they were a part of her Vegas residency, Siren's Song: The Hits of Tiffany Sharp. Tiffany had convinced them to learn new skills for a couple of songs because she wanted to incorporate aerial gymnastics. The show was scheduled to open in less than two months. Right now, they were practicing before rehearsal to avoid the judgmental stares of the more experienced aerial gymnasts and their trainer.

Emi seemed like a natural at silks. So did Jade, but she also excelled at grousing.

"No way," Amber said. "Lyra's not so bad."

The women turned to look as a door in the back of the auditorium opened. The first of the other performers had arrived. "It's showtime," Jade said with a grim smile.

"That went well."

Jade sniffed her disagreement at Emi's halfhearted assertion as they walked into their shared dressing room, followed by Amber and Caitlyn. Caitlyn closed the door and sank into a chair in front of the mirror. Her flushed face stared back, framed by a cloud of frizzy stray hairs.

"I'm not sure what my favorite part was." Amber sat beside her, undoing her braid until it fell in enviable waves down her back. "Getting stepped on by the brute in the stringer tank or told I might have a future as a human pretzel by Mademoiselle Dubois."

"It's zee easiest beginner transition," Jade mimicked the trainer's haughty French accent. She held out a hand, thumb pressed against forefinger, and gestured emphatically as she said, "But still, you struggle."

"You started out okay," Amber said, "but you slipped into Italian by the end."

"I'm a dancer, not an actress," Jade said. "And apparently even that's up for debate according to Mademoiselle Dubois and Natasha."

"If it makes you feel any better, nobody did that great today," Emi said. "Did you notice Tiffany completely forgot the choreo to part of 'Under Your Spell' as if we didn't perform it every night on tour?"

"We didn't even change any of the steps," Jade agreed. "She's really off her game."

"Too many late nights with Randy, no doubt." Amber grinned. "Right, Cat? Cat?"

"Looks like she's asleep sitting up again," Jade said.

"With her eyes open?" Emi asked.

Caitlyn realized everyone was staring at her. "Sorry, all the talk about pretzels made me hungry. Now all I can think about is the beer cheese at the Wild Hunt Steakhouse."

"Aren't you sick of hotel food?" Jade asked.

"Not this hotel," Caitlyn said.

"We haven't been there in a week," Emi said. "And it is dinner time."

"I could eat," Amber said. "Jade?"

"Fine." Jade reached for her towel and water. "I don't feel like driving anywhere anyway."

The perks of being a backup singer and dancer for Tiffany Sharp included free room and board at Avalon, and discounted meals on top of their regular pay. Caitlyn's suite made the guest room she often used at Tiffany's Hollywood home look modest in comparison: a living room including a kitchen and dining area, a large bedroom with a king-sized bed, picture windows, and a walk-in closet. There was a bathroom with marble tiles and counters, a walk-in shower, and a huge jacuzzi bathtub that made her painfully aware of being single.

Caitlyn stood in front of the mirror in the bathroom, scowling at her reflection as she brushed her frizzy hair. She wished she had time to shower and start from scratch, but Emi had made their dinner reservation for five. The clock said it was four-thirty the last time she looked at her phone. Another twenty-five minutes passed by the time she decided on a silky black tank dress to wear before slipping her feet into ballet flats. Caitlyn cursed the very fabric of time and space as she hurried to the elevator.

The other three women had already been seated in a dark leather booth by the time Caitlyn arrived at the Wild Hunt Steakhouse. Amber's blond hair fell in soft waves down the back of her curve-hugging jumpsuit. Emi had redone her ponytail, wisps of black hair framing her delicate face. Jade's longer, sleeker ponytail accented her high cheek bones and full lips. Her dark eyes flashed as she spoke to the other two in a hushed voice. Like Caitlyn, Jade wore a black dress, only hers was strapless, and she'd chosen flats instead of her usual stilettos.

"Something wrong?" Caitlyn asked as she slid into the booth beside Jade.

"*Meirda*, Cat," Jade swore under her breath, visibly startled. "How many times have I told you to start wearing a bell around your neck?"

"They found another dancer in a back alley on the old strip," Emi told Caitlyn, toying with the thin gold chain around her neck.

"Dead?" Caitlyn asked.

"Slit throat," Amber said. "Same as the other two. No evidence of, well…you know," Amber's voice trailed off.

"The authorities still won't confirm it's the same killer," Jade said.

"That's horrible," Caitlyn said, "but I don't think we have anything to worry about, at least. He seems preoccupied with Fremont Street." Her fellow dancers gave her sharp looks. "I mean, obviously it still sucks for the victims and anyone else who works there," she quickly amended.

A waitress appeared, rescuing Caitlyn from the awkward silence that followed as she set three drinks down on the table. "I see the fourth has arrived. Can I start you off with something to drink?"

"A Moscato, I guess." Caitlyn's eyes widened. "Did everyone already order apps?"

"Jade remembered your pretzel," Emi assured her.

Jade waved Caitlyn off when she tried to thank her. "Just making things easier on the staff."

Caitlyn's smile faded as she gazed at a mural of unearthly luminescent beings riding white elk and stranger beasts. They chased frightened people with wide eyes and mouths open in silent screams. Interesting aesthetic choice for someone trying to reassure real people the Fae meant them no harm, Caitlyn mused.

"Do you think that's why Tiffany seemed off at rehearsal today?"

Caitlyn didn't even realize she'd asked the question aloud until she noticed everyone staring.

"The killings, I mean."

The other women frowned. Even Jade looked nervous.

"She said she hasn't been sleeping well," Emi said, toying with her necklace again. "Nightmares or something. I'm sure she'll be better tomorrow."

After dinner, everyone decided to go to the most exclusive of three nightclubs in Avalon. The Grotto resembled an enchanted moonlit forest. Fairy lights flickered in bushes painted on the walls and on the ceiling above. The VIP booths along the side sat beneath realistic willow trees with leaves and more fairy lights hanging down instead of curtains.

The DJ and some of the bartenders wore only light brown suede pants, leather boots, and horns like satyrs. Cocktail waitresses and other bartenders wore brown suede corsets over white peasant blouses, green miniskirts, and floral wreaths instead. Dancers in green bikinis and wings equipped with glimmering LED lights shimmied atop a couple pillars on the edge of the dance floor.

"It's like Disneyland for grownups," Emi had observed the first night they ventured into the opulent nightclub.

Caitlyn often wondered how many employees were humans in Fae costumes, and how many were Fae using their gift of illusion to resemble humans in Fae costumes. The real Fae didn't have pointy ears like the nightclub staff wore, but their skin was translucent and appeared almost blue in its natural state, their eyes as black and fathomless as great white sharks. She shivered as she sat across from Amber and Jade beside Emi in their reserved VIP booth, another perk as part of Tiffany's entourage.

"I think I'm gonna call it an early night," Jade shouted over the throbbing baseline of electronic dance music. "My feet are killing me."

"Want me to come with you?"

Jade shook her head at Amber. "Stay. Have fun!"

Amber and Emi stayed for another half hour or so. Caitlyn switched to water after her one and only drink, but continued dancing until the crowd started to thin. She left the club behind a group of people that filled the first elevator to arrive.

Caitlyn had the next elevator to herself until a few gamblers entered at the next floor. They paid her no attention, and soon Caitlyn had the elevator to herself once more. As the elevator rose, Caitlyn found herself remembering a game she used to play with a childhood friend during sleepovers. They'd have ten seconds to bolt from the living room to the bedroom and shut the door before the "bad man" (whoever that was) got them. When the elevator reached her floor, Caitlyn made it to her suite in five.

chapter three

"Do you want to ask them to join us?"

Tiffany sat with Randy in a secluded booth in an alcove of the Wild Hunt. She had been watching through the railing as some of her dancers walked to a booth in the restaurant below. Tiffany turned to Randy. He wore a black dress shirt that was one undone button away from being scandalous tucked into dark jeans.

"I doubt they want to see any more of me after today's rehearsal. I'm asking them to learn all these new skills while I stumble through old dance routines," Tiffany said. "I even tripped over my own feet during 'Under Your Spell.' Then I forgot the words to the bridge. At least we're still using prerecorded music until we get the blocking down, so I don't think anyone noticed."

"Maybe I kept you up too late." Randy said it with a smile, but his amber eyes appeared concerned. "I should have slept on the couch instead of waking you up."

"I was having bad dreams, remember?" Tiffany smiled. "You did me a favor."

"Here's to getting a head start on better dreams tonight." Randy raised a glass of red wine.

Tiffany lifted her own to clink against his.

. . .

Less than a week later, Tiffany awoke to see a grim-faced Randy looking down at his phone. "Another one?" She sat up, her brow furrowed in dismay. "They really need a stronger police presence on Fremont Street."

"Not Fremont Street this time," Randy said. He showed Tiffany his phone.

Her eyes widened as she read the headline. "That's just a couple blocks away."

"Law enforcement will be spread even thinner if he's expanding his hunting grounds beyond the old strip," Randy said, "but they haven't ruled out a copycat killer. Before now, all the killings were at least a week apart."

"Maybe he's getting more confident." Tiffany shivered. "I want to see Morgan. Now." She climbed out of bed to exchange her thin camisole for a more supportive white tank top from the top drawer of her dresser. Then she pulled on a gray oversized sweatshirt. Tiffany searched in another drawer for a pair of black capri tights.

"What about rehearsal?" Randy rose and crossed the room to stand beside Tiffany.

Tiffany glanced at the alarm clock. "It's early," she said. "I've got time."

"I'm not sure what her schedule looks like for today," Randy said, "but I'm sure she's on top of things." He squeezed Tiffany's shoulder.

She laid her hand over top of his. "I'm sure she is, but I'd be remiss if I didn't speak to her on behalf of my dancers. Their safety is my number one priority. That, and based on past experience, I'm surprised the media hasn't tried to link anything to the Fae."

"Understood," Randy said. He pulled away from Tiffany and strode purposefully toward the bedroom door.

"Uhm, Randy?" Tiffany bit her lip on a smile.

He turned to look at her with a quizzical expression, tilting his head to one side.

"You might want to put some clothes on first."

Randy looked down. "Oh. Right."

Tiffany and a fully clothed Randy rode the elevator down to a level only reachable with a special access code. She thought it strange that Morgan granted her the top floor of Avalon while choosing to reside in the dark recesses of the resort instead, but Tiffany appreciated the generosity. Perhaps the Fae queen felt more secure underground.

After what felt like an impossibly long ride, the elevator arrived at the lowest level of Avalon. Randy had to input another code to open a door leading into a long hallway. The only source of light came from overhead LED track lighting. Morgan preferred soft lavender lighting to harsh fluorescents. The effect was cozy, if a little eerie.

Randy led Tiffany down the hall to Morgan's office. To their surprise, the door was ajar. Randy paused, holding a finger to his lips. Tiffany listened. Inside, Morgan was talking to someone. She sounded tense but not frightened.

"I'm sure it's just a coincidence," Tiffany heard her say. "Why would one of the convicts venture anywhere near Mor...me? The smart thing to do is get off this dying rock and go to a whole other world entirely."

"And yet the parallels are too striking to ignore," said an unfamiliar male voice.

Tiffany glanced at Randy. He shrugged, looking as perplexed as she felt.

"Wait a minute," said the same voice.

A moment later, the door opened wider. A beautiful man with golden brown skin and tufts of blond hair cropped close to his scalp stood in the doorway with a bemused expression. He was shorter than Randy but almost as imposing and well-muscled in a black tank top and relaxed jeans. Though he had amber eyes like Randy's, they possessed none of the shapeshifter's animal ferocity yet shared a certain intensity. If Tiffany didn't know better, she might have thought him an angel, the sort that would wield a flaming sword.

"Tiffany, darling, how long have you been waiting?"

Morgan slipped past the golden god to grasp one of Tiffany's hands and pull her into a spacious office with oak furniture and leather seating. Randy followed. The stranger took one last look in the hall before closing the door behind them.

The stranger gave a curt nod. "Randy."

"Hey, Lance. When did you get in town?"

"Early this morning."

Tiffany watched the exchange with mild interest, then turned back to Morgan. The Fae queen, wearing a shimmering burgundy camisole beneath a simple black suit, sat down behind a large desk. "You changed your hair." Tiffany felt foolish for stating the obvious as she sat across from the former redhead.

"What?" Morgan reached up to tuck a strand of curly black hair behind her ear. "Oh, I just wanted to mix things up a little."

"That's not Morgan," Randy said.

Morgan didn't argue. She merely pursed her lips and glanced at the man Randy called Lance with a look that appeared almost apologetic. He sighed, shaking his head.

"I knew something was off since the first time I smelled you," Randy continued. "I thought maybe it was just poor memory and the passage of time, but you never quite had a handle on your sister's mannerisms. Especially when you met with those mafiosos the other night."

Even her eyes were different, Tiffany realized. Brown instead of green. She rose from the chair, alarmed. "Vivienne," she breathed.

"Of course not, you ninny." Now Morgan—or whoever she was—stood, looking offended.

"That's Anna," said Lance.

"The baby sister," Randy explained.

"The *better* sister," said Anna.

"So, where the hell is Morgan?" Tiffany asked, bewildered.

Anna looked at her, dark eyes bleak. "We don't know."

"How long has she been missing?"

"We don't have an exact timeline," Lance said. "Morgan has always kept her own counsel, so it's not like we had regularly scheduled meetings. But we think she went M.I.A. sometime between the dragon incident in New York...and before you met her." He looked at Tiffany.

Tiffany turned from him to Anna. "It's been you this whole time?"

Anna nodded.

"I never did understand how a casino fit into Morgan's plans," Tiffany said. "What kind of game are you playing at?"

"It's no game," Anna sniffed. "Avalon was always a part of the plan. So were you."

"Morgan found out the previous hotel and casino had been built atop a large vortex," Lance said. "With humans learning more about the existence of other worlds, she didn't want to risk the land falling into the wrong hands. That, and casinos can be pretty lucrative under the right management. The Lafayette Foundation could certainly use the extra funds for legal fees."

"Morgan and I have different ideas about how to help the children of your world," Anna said, "but I don't want her foster homes shut down."

"Neither do I," Tiffany said, "but I still don't see where I fit into her plans."

"The Daughters of Morgan are spread a little thin," Lance said. "We all are, especially with smaller points of weakness opening up across the globe. Morgan probably intended for you to watch over the vortex here. I suspect there's more to it, but as long as she is missing, anything else is pure speculation."

"This vortex," Randy interrupted. "Do you think a certain escaped convict is utilizing it?"

"I was wondering how long the two of you were listening," Lance said. "And doubtful. It's covered by ten feet of cement. We don't even know where it leads, but Morgan didn't want to take any chances when she started construction of the new resort."

"But you share my suspicions that the Fremont Street killer is Convict Two."

"I'm leaning in that direction" Lance said. "Anna remains unconvinced, but some of our best agents are on the way."

"Some of your *only* agents." Anna appeared uncharacteristically glum.

Then again, Tiffany didn't know what Anna was really like, did she?

Before now, she'd known her only as Morgan le Fay.

"What are you thinking?" Randy said as he stopped outside the Otherworld Theatre.

Tiffany sighed. "I don't know, but I bet everyone will have a lot of questions if the killer has moved on to targeting women closer to home. And it looks like he's one of the Fae after all, so that's going to be a public relations nightmare if word gets out."

"Just tell them the truth," Randy said. "Not about Convict Two, obviously, but at least you can assure them Avalon's security team is aware of the risks and bringing in reinforcements to keep everyone safe."

"Sure," Tiffany said, unconvinced.

"If it makes you feel better, I'm going to touch base with Lance again later to reevaluate existing security systems. Alarms, cameras, all that. I thought about hanging around backstage, but so far all of the attacks have been outside bars and hotels."

Tiffany nodded. "I'm probably overreacting. I can't imagine a safer place in Vegas than where we are now."

Apart from being built on top of a big vortex, she reminded herself.

But no faeries or gloppy green monsters were breaking through ten feet of concrete.

chapter four

Caitlyn stood between Jade and Amber while Tiffany addressed two dozen dancers and aerial gymnasts.

"Morgan le Fay is increasing security to keep us safe in the resort and parking garage," Tiffany said, "but it's also important to use the buddy system. Nobody should travel to and from Avalon alone." She paused while the performers exchanged worried glances and murmurs. "If you need transportation, we can make safe arrangements for you. Please don't be afraid to ask. Now let's see if we can do a full run-through without any hiccups. My goal is to be ready for crew and a live band in the next week or so."

Amber reached for Caitlyn's hand. Caitlyn gave it a reassuring squeeze.

"We got this," Emi said under her breath.

Caitlyn felt a surge of relief when the final song ended after a full run-through of the show. Rehearsals were going better this week. Even Mademoiselle Dubois had nothing but praise for Amber and Caitlyn, Amber in particular. Despite their success, nobody felt like another evening out, so Caitlyn was on her own for dinner.

"Need a bag?" a bored clerk in a white blouse, suede vest, and dark pants asked. Even Avalon's self-contained convenience store, The

Enchanted Emporium, was on theme to resemble an outdoor market with green leaves and twinkling lights decorating all the shelves.

"Nah, I got it," Caitlyn said. She cradled a container of donuts, a loaf of bread, lunch meat, and sliced cheese with one arm.

The clerk looked doubtful as Caitlyn made a few clumsy attempts to form the handle on a thin cardboard box of soda. Triumphant, Caitlyn lifted the box with her free hand. The clerk remained unimpressed.

After she left the marketplace and hurried down the hallway to the elevator, Caitlyn ran into a man in a black suit, dropping everything but the soda. She knelt down to set the soda on the floor and pick up the other groceries.

"Here, let me help you with that," said a familiar voice.

Caitlyn found herself gazing at her reflection in the man's sunglasses as he handed her the donuts. She knew that blond buzz cut anywhere. "Agent Baker, we have got to stop running into each other like this." She stood with her groceries once again balanced precariously on her arm. "Someone might think we're in love."

Agent Baker sighed. "If I tell you why I'm here, do you promise to go away and stay out of trouble? It doesn't concern you this time, at least I bloody well hope not."

"Been in England lately?" Caitlyn raised an eyebrow.

"My mission has taken me all over the globe," Agent Baker said. "I was trying to find Convict Two in London. He, ah, has a history there. An informant based in London pointed me in the direction of Paris. Turns out he meant the Vegas hotel, not the city in France. I was really looking forward to a proper le pain du chocolat."

"Convict Two, huh?" Caitlyn knelt back down in an attempt to retrieve her soda. "What'd he do?"

"Nothing you need to worry about," Agent Baker said. "I'll get that."

Caitlyn rose unsteadily to her feet. "Don't suppose you can help me to my suite?"

Agent Baker frowned. "Ah...Morgan doesn't want me to attract any more attention to my presence than I already have, especially in her own hotel." He handed Caitlyn the soda.

"Fine," Caitlyn said. "Not like there's a killer in town targeting dancers or anything," she muttered under her breath.

Agent Baker's face remained unreadable behind his dark glasses. "Goodnight, Caitlyn."

She sighed. "G'night, Agent B."

"Convict Two *is* the killer," Caitlyn blurted out as she spread mayonnaise on a slice of bread in the kitchen of her suite. She shivered from the realization. Never mind the inevitable public relations disaster, it would be next to impossible to catch someone who could change their appearance at will. Some of the Fae could even make themselves invisible.

Caitlyn's blood ran cold at the thought of an invisible assailant. She paused in the middle of making her sandwich to check the deadbolt on her front door. She even looked behind every thick velvety green curtain, under the bed, and in the bathroom. She was being silly, she knew. All the women had been attacked outside. Then again, until last night, all the women had worked in bars and hotels on Fremont Street.

While she ate at the small but elegant oak dining table, Caitlyn pulled out her phone to read every news story she could find on the killings. Authorities didn't know much, and most coworkers and acquaintances were hesitant to talk to the police. None of the victims had family in the area. At least one may have worked as an escort.

Caitlyn clicked on a link to a news conference that had aired earlier today.

"Some people think the Metro isn't taking these killings as seriously as they should due to the occupations of the victims," a reporter with a sleek black bob asked. "Is there a greater urgency now that the killer has moved on to employees of more upscale establishments?"

"We investigate all murders with the same urgency," said the police chief of the Las Vegas Metropolitan Police Department. He appeared middle-aged with tired eyes and graying hair. "Right now, existing evidence remains inconclusive that these murders are even connected. And unfortunately, some occupations carry greater risks than others. That's just the sad reality of the world we live in."

"If the murders *are* connected, that points to a serial killer, doesn't it?" asked another reporter, this one with unruly blond curls. His green eyes looked intense behind fashionable wire-framed eyeglasses. Unhappy murmurs spread throughout the crowd.

"Has the FBI gotten involved?" asked yet another reporter. "Concerned viewers have reported sightings of people in black suits and unmarked vehicles patrolling the area."

Caitlyn stopped the video. *FBI?* she wondered.

Or Agent Baker and company?

Something told her potential witnesses wouldn't be any more enthusiastic about talking to him than to the police. Not unless he disguised himself as another dancer. Caitlyn giggled at the thought of Agent Baker in gold sequined hotpants or maybe even disguised as a woman. Then she had another crazier thought and set down her phone.

Caitlyn walked into the kitchen and searched through a drawer until she found post it-notes and a pen. She sat back down at the dining table and started writing.

chapter five

Tiffany sat on the golden jacquard comforter that covered her bed and looked around the hotel room, feeling bored. Randy was off evaluating the resort's security systems with Lance as promised, so she was on her own. She realized she hadn't seen her other cat, Gizmo, a gray Devon rex with wild eyes, in days.

Tiffany leaned over the side of the bed and lifted the comforter. "You down there?"

"If you're looking for Gizmo, don't bother."

Tiffany sat up as something furry brushed against her arm.

"Pardon?" Tiffany looked at Groucho Manx in surprise. Surely the cat hadn't spoken.

"I said if you're looking for Gizmo, don't bother." Groucho Manx settled onto a pillow with a gold jacquard pillow sham, draping one front leg over the other. "He can smell Wolf Boy all over you. Probably hiding in your closet somewhere. Only comes out late at night or when the two of you are away."

Tiffany's eyes widened. "When did you learn how to talk? *How* do you talk?"

"I've always known how to talk, you self-absorbed potato." Groucho's green eyes flashed. "You never bothered to listen until now."

Tiffany still felt too surprised to take offense. She thought back on tonight's feast. Lobster grilled cheese, lobster bisque, a salad, and a bottle of white wine, of which she had only had a couple glasses. No berries or mushrooms or any other potentially sketchy ingredients unless someone from room service drugged her food or somehow spiked an unopen bottle of wine.

No, clearly the source of Tiffany's problem was internal.

"I'm having a nervous breakdown," she told Groucho. "Between the nightmares and the stress of the residency and a killer on the loose and all the other Fae business, is it any wonder I'm losing my mind? Who wouldn't go crazy?"

"Your mind may be broken," Groucho said, "but your hands still work. Would you mind scratching me behind my left ear? There's an itch I can't quite hit at the right angle."

Not knowing what else to do, Tiffany gave Groucho scritches as requested. His eyes closed in apparent ecstasy as he began to knead at the top of the pillow case.

"Oh, yeah...right there."

"Uhm, Groucho?"

"I'm making it weird, aren't I?"

"Lil' bit."

"I'm afraid I won't be very good company today," Randy told Tiffany when he walked into the bedroom the next morning, "but I brought you breakfast in bed. The Bluebelle Bakery really outdid themselves today. Honey-dipped donuts with lavender crème filling and these little unicorn sprinkles. Mmm." He waved a fragrant donut in front of Tiffany's face before returning it to a small white box with the Bluebelle Bakery logo in metallic blue. "Festive."

Tiffany forced a smile as she accepted the box from his outstretched hands.

"No more nightmares, I hope?" Randy slipped off his shoes, then sat beside Tiffany.

She shook her head as she took a bite of her donut. Her eyes closed as she savored it. Not too sweet with a hint of floral flavor. "It's so good."

Randy smiled. "You got a little something on your face." He gently brushed the corner of Tiffany's mouth with his thumb and leaned in to give her a kiss.

"Gross! What a cheeseball."

Groucho sat on the nightstand, watching. Tiffany looked over her shoulder and waved her free hand to shoo him away.

Groucho didn't budge.

Mercifully oblivious, Randy started to strip down to his boxers before climbing into bed beside Tiffany. "I plan to be up by dinnertime, but I'm going to spend the next couple of nights helping to patrol the parking garage in particular."

"You don't think anyone will notice a giant wolf lurking in the shadows?" Tiffany asked.

"I can be stealthy." Randy grinned.

Tiffany treated herself to a spa day with Jade and Amber while Randy slept. Emi had other plans, and nobody knew where Caitlyn had gone after Emi caught a glimpse of her at the breakfast buffet. Tiffany felt guilty. She hadn't spent a lot of time with Caitlyn outside of rehearsals. She decided to plan something special for just the two of them to catch up. Despite one hell of a misunderstanding when Tiffany blamed Caitlyn for Brendan's manipulations, Caitlyn had always been a good friend and she didn't hold a grudge.

Tiffany considered talking to Caitlyn about the Groucho Manx situation. She had hoped it was a one-time thing when she woke up this morning, just a momentary lapse in sanity, but nope, the cat still spoke. And he didn't even have anything nice to say.

Which came first, Tiffany wondered, *the name or the snark?*

She winced as the masseuse worked on a knot in her shoulder. "So tense," Kim said. "You need to come by more often." As short and as slight as the woman was, Kim had strong hands and a stern disposition to match. "No tears. You'll feel so much better when I'm done."

Morgan, or Anna—who knew where one sister's contribution ended and the other began—had outdone herself when it came to The Crystal Cavern. All the walls and the floor in the day spa shimmered with inlaid crystals. Realistic stalactites resembling amethyst and rose quartz hung from the high ceilings, but the effect felt more enchanting than claustro-phobic. The rooms were lit just enough to see comfortably. Unseen speakers played gentle music with angelic vocals. Tiffany saw no candles, incense, or wax warmers, but the rooms smelled of jasmine and sandal-wood. An informational pamphlet credited the spa's design to former Disney imagineers.

After her massage, Tiffany joined Jade and Amber in a room with a hot tub. The jewelblue water felt wonderful after Kim worked Tiffany's kinks out. Employees brought them mimosas with edible flowers in sturdy plastic flutes that resembled fine crystal. By the time they were done, Tiffany had learned about Jade's short-lived romance with a dealer at another resort. Amber's dating woes were because her parents wished her preferences were a little narrower than "gorgeous and talented," even though they tried to be supportive.

Tiffany tried to tell Jade and Amber as much as she could about Randy without giving away his secret—and forget about divulging her ongoing mental break. One way or another, she always had to keep walls up, now even with Randy.

That evening Randy announced his presence by tripping over Gizmo in the living room and swearing under his breath. The Devon rex had made a rare appearance when Tiffany sat down to order room service. She was debating whether or not to ask him if he'd like to talk when he bolted off the couch and under Randy's feet. *Just as well*, she decided.

"I'm thinking surf and turf tonight," Tiffany said. "I still have half a bottle of Pinot Grigio left, but maybe we should get something red, too."

"Sounds good, but I have to pass on the wine," Randy said. "Garage duty, remember?"

"Oh. Right." Tiffany frowned. She realized she'd barely thought about the killings all day. Her stomach turned as she remembered.

Randy sat beside Tiffany. "It'll be okay," he said, putting an arm around her shoulder. "We've caught him before. We'll get him again. Hopefully before he can hurt anyone else."

"Yeah," Tiffany said, "I just wish…well, I wish things had gone differently. Like, he never escaped, but you and my father still did, or maybe it would have been better if my father never did, either. Or…" She trailed off.

"I understand," Randy said, pulling her closer. "No sense dwelling on the past. We can only move forward with the knowledge we have now, and hope things go better in the future. More agents arrived yesterday. I'm 99.9% sure Agent Baker won't try to blame me this time."

Tiffany laughed. Then she straightened. "Randy, I know we've talked about this before, but when you told me my dad could communicate with other animals, how did it work? Like, was he just really insightful about animal behavior, or did they actually…you know…talk?"

If Randy thought it was a weird question, he didn't say so aloud. Instead, he told her, "You know, I never really asked specifics. But it didn't seem any stranger than the Fae's illusions, and I'd witnessed those firsthand."

"And I suppose a glamour that makes someone look different seems pretty mundane when you can literally transform into something different," Tiffany said.

"Right," Randy agreed. "Anyway, I think I assumed a telepathic link more so than actual conversation. I already knew they can read human thoughts. And sometimes my own if I'm not careful to guard my mind. Why not other animals?"

Tiffany considered telling Randy about Groucho Manx.

"Why do you ask?" Randy peered at her face.

Tiffany hesitated. She couldn't do it. Not yet.

"No reason. Sometimes I wonder why the Fae acquired their psychic abilities in the first place, I guess. Is it some sort of natural adaptation? Do telepathy and mind control help them catch food in their own world?"

Randy considered. "Like the obvious benefits of turning into a wolf or calling upon the elements? When you put it that way, all the visitors to your world sound uniquely built for predation." He gave Tiffany a rueful grin, a shock of auburn hair falling over one eye.

"I think humans have always used our intellect to develop better weapons above more altruistic ends. We destroy as much as we create, and so much of what we create destroys. I can't imagine how much worse we would be with real superpowers." An awful thought occurred to Tiffany as she considered the psychic abilities of the Fae. "My father…do you think he used mind control on my mother?"

Randy looked taken aback. "No. I think he was considerate of how he used his abilities, even with other animals, just like Morgan and Lance… and Anna, I presume. And if you develop any latent Fae abilities, I know you can be trusted not to abuse them. But don't underestimate your existing talents. You already have the power to do much good."

Tiffany wasn't worried about abusing her newfound ability to communicate with other animals, but she couldn't think of any practical uses for it, either. She sighed and looked across the room. Groucho was sleeping in an armchair, mercifully quiet.

chapter six

Caitlyn liked to relax and take it easy most days off, but not today. She had dressed comfortably in a baggy white tee, blue running shorts, and sneakers. Her hair was pulled back into a single braid and tucked under a baseball cap. After eating a donut and checking her face for any traces of powdered sugar, Caitlyn headed downstairs to the resort lobby. Her phone beeped to notify her a driver named Jenna had arrived in a white Kia sedan.

As she stepped out into the sweltering July heat, Caitlyn saw the car up the street ahead of a line of taxis and other ride-sharing vehicles. Not even noon, and already a bead of sweat snaked down the side of her face. New York City could be miserable in the summer, and so could Los Angeles, but neither compared to July in Las Vegas.

A tall athletic woman with dark brown skin and short black hair exited the sedan to let Caitlyn into the back passenger seat. "Feels like another miserable day of record-breaking heat," Jenna said as she sat back down in the driver's seat. "Hope your plans include swimming. Fremont Street's a lot more fun at night. Have you seen the light show?"

"Not yet," Caitlyn said.

"Are you meeting anyone there?"

Caitlyn knew Jenna was just making polite conversation, but she shifted uncomfortably. "I have a lot of people to see today," she answered truthfully.

"Well, if you plan on staying late, make sure you stick with friends," Jenna advised. "My shift ends in a few hours, but if you see a 'Kim' or a 'Stacy' available, they're my girls. Both drive Hondas. They can get you home safely." She smiled at Caitlyn in the rearview mirror.

"Thanks," Caitlyn said, smiling back.

Jenna dropped Caitlyn off by the Fremont Street Parking Garage at the corner of Carson and Fourth Street. Fremont Street was already crowded with pedestrians despite the early hour and the heat. A shaggy-haired busker grinned when Caitlyn dropped a couple dollars into his worn leather guitar case. He began to strum "Pretty Woman" as she walked to her first stop.

Her parents loved that old song. They had danced to it at their wedding —because "Smells Like Teen Spirit" didn't seem like an appropriate choice, her father would kid as he reminisced about the past. He even chose it as the soundtrack to a slideshow at her mother's funeral—and for the same reason, he'd later say with a sad smile.

A flash of gold in the distance caught Caitlyn's attention.

Boy, I hope she remembered sunblock, Caitlyn thought as she watched a pale, scantily clad woman promote a two-story club from the balcony. Apparently, pasties were sufficient to evade public decency charges on Fremont Street. Already Caitlyn sensed a very different vibe from the more family-friendly walk along the newer strip, reinforced by a rowdier crowd. She couldn't imagine what happened after sunset.

Someone hooted overhead. Caitlyn looked up to see a man zipline over Fremont Street, his arms stretched out like Superman. She turned back in the direction of the woman in the gold sequined pasties. That club was Caitlyn's first stop. She passed under Vegas Vic, a neon cowboy in front of the Pioneer Club, and crossed to the other side.

Caitlyn walked inside a smaller club neighboring the lounge Vic's "girl-friend" Vickie now called home. She walked up a set of carpeted stairs that led to the upstairs bar. Fans whirled overhead and misters lined the balcony. Most of the chairs and sofas were unoccupied. Caitlyn sat in a chair in the farthest corner of the balcony, enjoying the feel of the mist against her face. A cocktail waitress wearing little more than the go-go dancer approached. She sounded disappointed when Caitlyn asked for only a soda.

"I'm here for an interview," Caitlyn said.

"Sure thing, hon. I'll be right back with your drink." The waitress twirled a blond pigtail around her finger and shimmied as she walked away, to the appreciative stares of middle-aged men in business suits and younger tourists.

What a life, Caitlyn thought. Her eyes returned to the go-go dancer, who set down her sign and picked up a short red satin robe from a chair.

Caitlyn hoped she kept her expression neutral as the dancer approached her, tying the belt of her robe. "I'm Quinn. You Candy?" the dancer said as she sat in the chair across from Caitlyn. She stretched out her long legs and propped her feet on the ottoman between them. "Real name or stage name?"

Up close, Caitlyn could see a hint of crows' feet in the corner of the woman's face. "Re...real," Caitlyn stammered, taken aback by the women's dry tone.

"Sure, it is." The woman tilted her head as she examined Caitlin. Her hair fell in soft brown curls, but her face remained hard and impassive. "You're gonna need to get over your shyness before you even think of a job like this." She waggled her fingers in Caitlyn's general direction.

"I'm not...it's just—I'm from the Northeast," Caitlyn explained, removing her hat and pushing back her sunglasses. "Still adjusting to the heat."

"My boss said you wanted to talk to one of us first because you had some questions about the work. Not the sort of request I'd expect her to entertain, but we're short on dancers, especially after..." Quinn trailed off.

"Regina Blake," Caitlyn said. "It's awful what happened to her. That's sort of why I had some...reservations, I guess."

"I always told her to have one of the bouncers walk her back to her car, but Regina was fearless. You have to be in this line of work, but you gotta be smart, too. Don't get me wrong. She was putting herself through med school. Wanted to be a pediatrician." A smile softened her features, then her blue eyes flashed. "And those cops had the nerve to ask if she was hustling for other work on the side. Believe it or not, we run a clean operation here."

"Good to know," Caitlyn said. "So, you don't think it was a customer."

"Who knows." Quinn shrugged. "You got any more questions, or can I get back to work?"

Caitlyn still had plenty of questions when she left the club, and very few answers. She wasn't even sure what kind of clues she was looking for. She just knew she couldn't sit and wait until the killer struck again. Not after everything she knew about the Fae. She had time before her next meeting, so Caitlyn bought loaded nachos and a frozen lemonade for lunch.

After finding a suitably shady table, Caitlyn sat down to eat and people-watch. The performance art dancers, as she learned they were called instead of go-go dancers, included scantily clad men—some wearing little more than G-strings.

Equal opportunity objectification, she decided. *Neat!*

Caitlyn finished her food. Her search for a garbage can brought her to her next stop. She decided to check out the back alley of the hotel where a restaurant employee had found the second victim. Caitlyn hadn't seen a point of investigating the parking garage where Regina's body was found. Even the alley would have been scrubbed for all evidence by now, but maybe having a better sense of Fremont Street's back alleyways would benefit her investigation.

Caitlyn wished she'd spent more time watching those police procedurals her parents liked as she walked behind the hotel. *Dumb*, she told herself. *It's entertainment, not a field manual.*

Still, her experience with Quinn taught her she needed to do a better job of playing the part of a dancing hopeful. Surely watching more crime dramas would have aided her performance. Or maybe she could draw on actual lived experience as a dancer instead of playing detective.

"So dumb," Caitlyn said aloud.

"Excuse me?"

Caitlyn came to a stop in the alley. A young man scraping food off dishes into a foul-smelling dumpster looked at her, raising an eyebrow. He had unruly red hair and freckles, and looked more startled to see Caitlyn than she was to see him.

"Sorry," she said. "I was just…"

"Talking to yourself?" he offered.

"I'm not crazy, I swear."

"Right." He sounded unconvinced. "So why are you back here?"

Caitlyn decided to stick with the truth. He looked like he was about twelve, so really, what could he possibly do with the information?

"Investigating," she said.

Now he looked more annoyed than worried. "Oh God, you're not another one of those weirdo true crime podcasters, are you?"

"What-casters? No!" Caitlyn removed her sunglasses. She fought the urge to giggle at the way he grasped his plate and rubber spatula in front of him like a shield and sword. "I'm so sorry. You weren't the one who found Tammy Harris, were you?"

"I replaced the guy who did," the busboy said. "They were dating. Cops tried to blame him, but the whole kitchen could vouch for him because we do a late-night menu on weekends." Then, perhaps deciding he'd said too much, he added, "I think you should go."

Caitlyn stifled another giggle as the busboy gestured with his spatula for emphasis. She didn't find him particularly intimidating, but the smell coming out of the dumpster made her feel ill. She turned around and left the alley.

"I called earlier about the opening for the dancing dealer position?"

The hostess, a pretty girl in a black minidress, nodded. "Marty's the manager on duty right now. I'll see if he's available to speak with you. You can wait over there." She gestured to an elegant bench near the hostess stand. Caitlyn sat. She watched as the hostess approached a tall muscular man with a white-collared shirt, rolled up high enough to accentuate his large biceps, and black dress pants.

A red-haired employee had followed him out of the kitchen. His eyes widened when the hostess pointed in Caitlyn's direction. He said something to Marty.

Caitlyn sat frozen like a deer in headlights as Marty strode across the restaurant into the lobby. "You need to show yourself out before I help you out," he growled at her. "And tell your boss over at the Gazette to stop playing games. We're done answering any questions."

chapter seven

After Caitlyn made a graceless exit from the hotel restaurant, she considered giving up her investigation altogether. At least Marty appeared to mistake her for a professional journalist, and not a podcaster, whatever the hell that was. *Must be like a YouTuber*, she decided, recalling her short-lived role as Tiffany's personal assistant.

Caitlyn was definitely better at singing and dancing than being a personal assistant or a private detective, but she chose to follow through with her last appointment anyway. If she fell during a show, she just had to pick herself back up and keep going.

It's just another performance; she reminded herself as she walked to an open-air bar on the other end of Fremont Street. Even the bartenders and wait staff put on a show in this town. She sat at a round high-top table in the island-themed bar and watched as bartenders juggled glasses and performed tricks while they mixed drinks. Caitlyn noticed one bartender in particular looked awfully familiar, but before she could take another peek at his face, a woman with a black fishtail braid sat across from her. Crystals accented her glittery eye makeup that somehow remained in flawless condition despite the heat. She wore a shimmering leotard.

"Hi, I'm Selina. Crystal, right?"

"Right," Caitlyn lied. "I'm sorry about Angel."

"She was such a beautiful soul," Selina said, eyes downcast. "Perfect name for aerial gymnastics. Everybody thought it was a stage name, but her given name was Angelina, and she'd gone by Angel ever since we were kids."

Caitlyn felt taken aback. "You grew up together?"

Selina nodded, smiling. "We used to tell everyone we were sisters, even though her parents are Albanian. Best friend I ever had."

Caitlyn didn't know what to say.

"So, tell me about you," Selina said. "What's your favorite apparatus?"

"Lyra," Caitlyn told her.

"Me, too. Angel mostly performed on the trapeze, but I'm not sure if José is ready for a new partner yet." Selina peered at Caitlyn's face. "How much trapeze experience do you have? Have you done any partner work?"

"I, uhm, wow. Let me think." Caitlyn realized she should have anticipated Selina's questions and planned her answers ahead of time.

"Take off your sunglasses," Selina said.

"What?" Caitlyn stared at her in surprise, but took them off and set them on the table. She watched with growing unease as Selina took a phone out and started typing. When the gymnast found what she was looking for, she hit play and held out the phone.

"This you?" she demanded.

Even without sound, Caitlyn recognized the music video for "Under Your Spell."

"So what?" Selina continued without waiting for an answer. "Did Tiffany Sharp cut you from her residency at Avalon? Come to slum it with us here on the old strip? Why lie and use a fake name? Can you even do aerial gymnastics?"

"Tiffany didn't cut me," Caitlyn said. "I just…I wanted to help."

"No, you wanted to be nosy," Selina said, putting away her phone. "If it isn't law enforcement accusing us of sex work—which, totally valid, but not my vibe—it's YouTube makeup artists and podcasters using us for internet clout…and apparently crummy backup dancers like you are getting in on the grift now, too, for some dumbass reason."

"I really am sorry about your friend," Caitlyn tried to say, but Selina was already rising from the table.

"We're done here."

"Well, that was embarrassing for you," said a male voice behind Caitlyn after Selina stormed off.

"As embarrassing as a former Broadway performer slinging drinks in Vegas?" Caitlyn turned to face former castmate Nick Pagonis. "I thought that was you." She noted the way his dark hair reached the collar of his black button-down shirt. It was soft, too, she remembered. Her cheeks reddened.

"Wow. I don't remember you being a mean girl. That was more Anne Marie's thing," he said, but his green eyes looked more amused than offended. "You never did call me after that night at the club."

Caitlyn remembered that night more vividly than she preferred. Especially the look on her ex-boyfriend's face when he saw her sitting in Nick's lap. A jolt of aggravation interrupted her feelings of guilt and regret. "You never called me, either," she said.

Nick laughed. "It's not that serious," he said. "What are you up to, anyway?"

Caitlyn sighed. "I was trying to investigate the murders."

"Didn't you end up unconscious and bleeding the last time you played detective?"

Caitlyn's jaw dropped. "What? No!"

It wasn't a lie. Technically, NYC was the first time Caitlyn investigated anything but not the last. And she'd never lost consciousness when she helped Tiffany in L.A. despite an unfortunate tumble down some stairs. There may have been some blood, but nothing bad enough to warrant so much as a bandage. With a start, Caitlyn realized Nick was still speaking.

"—according to Max. Anyway, I hope the angry lady was wrong, and this isn't your new side hustle. Sounds like a bad TV series. Caitlyn Smith," Nick said mockingly, "dancer by night, dick by day."

"Better than being a dick all the time," Caitlyn muttered under her breath.

"What?"

"Better go. I'm running out of time."

And patience.

Of all the luck, bumping into Nick here. The world was starting to feel a little too small for Caitlyn's comfort level. She turned and walked away, certain she could still feel the heat of his stare until she left the open-air bar.

· · ·

After her ill-fated encounter with Nick, Caitlyn stopped walking down Fremont Street to look at an electronic billboard announcing a new surprise addition to tonight's Downtown Rocks, Fire and Ash. The band had opened for Tiffany on the US leg of her last tour. Like Tiffany, the singer and bassist were former residents of a Lafayette Foundation foster home.

Her world just kept getting smaller and smaller.

At least Caitlyn liked the band. And things with the guitarist, Ben, had ended amicably enough after a few exploratory dates on the road. She wondered if Tiffany knew Fire and Ash was in town. She pulled out her phone to send a text.

Within moments, Tiffany replied, *Are you still there? Let's meet up.*

Caitlyn hadn't planned on staying, but she decided to make an exception for Tiffany. After all, they'd be safe if they stuck together. Not that Caitlyn was worried about her safety, but Nick had raised a valid point, as much as she loathed to admit it.

There's an open-air tiki bar near the main stage, she started to text back.

No, Caitlyn decided, deleting her text. *Not there.* She walked back in the direction of the main stage and saw another open-air bar across from Nick's work, this one decorated with venetian masks and beads instead of tiki masks and torches. Every day could be Mardi Gras on Fremont Street, apparently.

Something else caught her attention after she typed directions to Tiffany. A group of people had gathered around a busker. She walked closer. This guy didn't play an instrument. Instead, he appeared to pass a ball of fire from one hand to the other. He produced a second, then a third, spinning them from one hand to the other like the antagonist in one of Caitlyn's favorite old movies juggled glass orbs.

Sleight of hand, or something more?

Caitlyn remembered the elementalists who'd helped hold Tiffany captive in Los Angeles. One was a pyromancer, but both had died. They were also large powerful men, but this dark-haired kid looked no older than eighteen. Lean and muscular in his black tank top and jeans, he worked the crowd with a magician's grace.

But this…this is the real deal, Caitlyn thought as she watched him manipulate the flames.

The kid caught her eye and winked.

Then he tossed each fiery orb into the air and appeared to swallow them one by one before retrieving a baseball cap filled with cash. Caitlyn decided to follow as he darted off, to the dismay of his enthusiastic audience. She doubted he had anything to do with the killer, but if there were elementalists in town, Tiffany and Morgan le Fay needed to know about it. At least her clumsy investigation wouldn't be a complete waste if she discovered something useful.

Fremont Street had grown a lot busier as evening approached. Caitlyn's stomach growled, but she ignored it as she tried to keep pace with the kid. He deftly slipped through the crowd, widening the distance. Caitlyn closed the gap when the kid paused at a street vendor to buy a couple hot dogs. Instead of finding a place to sit, he ducked down a dark alleyway. She followed, grateful for the noise of the crowd that covered the sound of her footsteps.

"C'mon," Caitlyn heard a male voice say as she crouched near the alley, obscured by a row of garbage cans and recycling bins.

"I'm sick of hot dogs," said a much younger female voice.

Caitlyn slowly worked her away to the edge of the wall and peered into the alley. The kid knelt in front of a little girl with the same curly dark hair, only longer and pulled back into a messy ponytail. She wore a big tee shirt like a dress.

Something beeped loudly. The kid and the little girl turned in Caitlyn's direction. She hoped she moved before they saw her. "Damn phone," she muttered under her breath as she pulled her smartphone out of the pocket in her shorts.

Where R U?!

Oops. Caitlyn had forgotten all about Tiffany. She rose to her feet and risked another look into the alley. Both the kid and the little girl were gone. *Where do they live?* Caitlyn wondered. *Are they homeless?*

Uncertain what to make of things, she replied to Tiffany's text and started walking back to their meeting place.

chapter eight

Tiffany sat in the Carnival Tavern, tapping her fingers anxiously on a small high-top table. She peered down Fremont Street for any sign of Caitlyn roaming the crowd, then stared at her phone. She considered getting up to look when dots appeared. *Finally.*

"Another water?" a bartender asked, sounding annoyed. She suspected the only reason the attractive, if stone-faced, man tolerated her presence so far was because he recognized her despite the oversized sunglasses and nondescript clothing, just a pink tee and jeans.

"Two," Tiffany told him. "And a menu. My friend's almost here."

She looked back down at her phone.

Sorry. OMW, Caitlyn had messaged. Then *Big news. Maybe.*

Tiffany didn't have time to puzzle the second message out because an out-of-breath Caitlyn was already sliding into the seat across from her. She reached for the frazzled woman's hand and squeezed. "Where were you? I was worried!"

Caitlyn looked surprised. "It's not even dark yet. I'm fine. But I saw something," she added in a lower voice. "An elementalist. At least I'm pretty sure he's an elementalist. That, or he's one hell of a magician, and Morgan should give him a gig at Avalon."

"An elementalist? Here?" Tiffany looked around as if one might materialize beside them. Only the grumpy bartender appeared, holding water and a menu.

"He was busking," Caitlyn explained. "And he's young. He finished working the crowd and bought food for himself and someone else, a little girl. I was...sort of spying on them in an alley when you messaged me. Should've had my phone on vibrate. They disappeared."

Worry gnawed at Tiffany's stomach. "Do you think they're after us," she asked, "because of what happened to the others in L.A.?"

"A couple of kids?" Caitlyn said. "I doubt it. He winked at me, but I don't think he knows who I am. Isn't their own world ending? What if they're brother and sister, and their parents died," Caitlyn continued with growing urgency. "Maybe they came here because they have nowhere else to go." Her eyes widened. "We should help them."

"I'll talk to A...Morgan," Tiffany said, inwardly cursing at herself for the near-slip. "One way or another, something needs to be done."

Caitlyn nodded, her eyebrows knitted together with apparent worry.

Tiffany and Caitlyn indulged in oysters, crab cakes, and mint juleps while the first act played. Once they'd eaten their fill of beignets for dessert, they left the open-air bar and navigated the crowd until they were close to the stage.

After the second band finished their set, efficient roadies in black Fire and Ash tees emblazoned with a phoenix began setting up. The brutal sun began to set as the band took the stage. The lead singer, Makayla Watson, opened the show with a surprising scream before launching into the band's newest single, "Living the Nightmare," the sort of pop-metal hybrid that defined their sound. A laser light show began overhead.

Tiffany snuck a peek at Caitlyn's face. She knew her friend had briefly dated the band's guitarist, Ben Baker, during the tour, but Caitlyn seemed perfectly content as she sang along with the chorus. A shock of dark hair with burgundy highlights obscured the face of the bassist, Izzy Rodrigues. Gavin, shirtless as always, appeared to be living his best life as he drummed away with dizzying intensity. It occurred to Tiffany that she still didn't know his last name. She decided to amend that if they had a chance to meet with the band after the show.

Now that the women had removed their sunglasses, Ben appeared to recognize them during the second song. He knelt on the stage in front of Caitlyn as he launched into a guitar solo. She cheered and clapped, delighted. Tiffany smiled.

Tiffany wasn't surprised to receive a text from Makayla when the band took a brief break after the first hour: *I should have messaged you before, but it was so last minute. Between taking a red eye and napping, I lost track of time. Hang with us after the show?*

"Up for meeting the band later?" Tiffany asked Caitlyn.

"Of course," she said, grinning.

We're in, Tiffany texted Makayla.

We have a corner suite on the top floor, Makayla replied. *I'll let the front desk know.*

"Ohmigosh, how've you been?" Makayla threw her arms around Tiffany as soon as Gavin opened the door to their opulent suite. She still wore the black minidress she wore on stage, her black hair falling in long braids. Gavin appeared more modest in a black tee and torn jeans in place of his skintight leather pants.

"Staying out of trouble?" Ben grinned at Caitlyn. He still wore the black tee he wore during the show, but he had traded his jeans for a pair of shorts.

"Not so much," Caitlyn said, smiling back.

I don't get it, Tiffany thought as she watched their easy banter while they sat together on a loveseat. Only Izzy appeared unhappy as she walked up to Makayla and held her smartphone.

"No more bad news," Makayla said. "My heart can't take it."

"What's going on?" Tiffany asked, sitting beside Makayla on the sofa. Izzy sat on the other side. Gavin stretched out across from Ben and Caitlyn in an oversized chair.

"Did you ever hear about that cult that was abducting kids on the east coast?" Makayla asked. "The one that tried to frame the Lafayette Foundation?"

Tiffany nodded. She wondered if Makayla and Izzy knew that the cult had "sacrificed" the children to Morgan's sister Anna, who rescued them instead and spirited them off to some other world to form their own secret utopia. Tiffany had only recently learned the truth herself. Aloud, Tiffany asked, "Didn't everyone involved get arrested?"

"Yes," Makayla said, "but they have really good lawyers. The lead guy, Emerson Fowler, the one whose son killed some women before he got eaten by reavers? He might get out on some stupid technicality. It's been all over the local news."

Tiffany's head spun as she took all the information in.

"That asshole was already gunning for the Lafayette Foundation before," Izzy said. "He knows Hannah had something to do with his son's death."

Hannah, Tiffany remembered, helped at the Lafayette home Izzy and Makayla grew up in. She was also a famed Daughter of Morgan, and the former lead singer of Fire and Ash before Makayla took her place. Tiffany wondered if Hannah knew her mother was missing, but she didn't want to say anything.

Ugh, what a mess.

"Not much we can do about it for now," Makayla said. "But enough about that creepy old man. How have things been with you?"

Everyone spent the next few hours catching up until Tiffany yawned loudly. Makayla called for a car to take Tiffany and Caitlyn back to Avalon. "The whole family's coming opening night, right?" Tiffany asked Makayla as she walked them down to the lobby.

"Are you kidding?" Makayla said. "The twins haven't shut up about it."

Tiffany hugged her. "If you need to talk to me…about anything," she said, "you know how to reach me. I may not be able to help, but I'm more than happy to listen."

"You should let Morgan know, too," Makayla said. "About what's happening back east. Assuming she doesn't already know. I'm dumb." She smacked her forehead. "Of course she knows. She's Morgan le Fay."

Tiffany nodded weakly.

"I don't get it," Tiffany said as she stood in the elevator with Caitlyn. "You and Ben seem perfect for each other. What went wrong?"

Caitlyn shrugged. "He's smart and he's funny, and I don't think he has a jealous streak like my ex, but I just didn't feel...I don't know—that spark. Maybe I'm holding out for something that doesn't even exist. Did Randy give you butterflies?"

"Still does," Tiffany said. She gave Caitlyn a sympathetic smile. "Good night," she said when the elevator stopped at Caitlyn's floor.

"G'night. Oh!" Caitlyn put a hand on the elevator door before it could close. "Don't forget to tell Morgan about the elementalists!"

And that creep in New York, Tiffany thought as the door closed. She had a lot to talk to Anna about. She worried Morgan's little sister might be as overwhelmed as the rest of them. *Living the nightmare, indeed.*

chapter nine

"Wake up, sleepyhead."

"Good morning," Tiffany said with a yawn. "I was just dreaming about you." Tiffany rolled over to look at Randy. Groucho Manx stared at her instead, his stubby tail twitching.

"I hope there was food in this dream," he said. "Gizmo's hungry, and so am I."

Tiffany sat up and stretched. "Thanks for not climbing on my face as per the usual."

"Seemed inappropriate," Grouch Manx said, "now that we can communicate like proper civilized adults and all. Why were you out so late, anyway? Bored of your boy toy already? Good riddance, I say. I know Gizmo wouldn't miss him."

"Catching up with friends," Tiffany said, rolling her eyes. "Have *you* ever had a friend?"

"Just Gizmo." Groucho Manx sighed. "He's not the most intellectually stimulating companion, but beggars can't be choosers. Now maybe if you let me roam around this hotel, I could make some new friends. Be your eyes and ears on the ground. I know you want intel. I can sneak into places your smelly boy toy can't."

"Absolutely not," Tiffany said. "I'm lucky Morgan even lets me have pets." She climbed out of bed and walked into the living room to fill the cats' food dish.

"Food, food, food, food, food," a wild-eyed Gizmo chanted as he ran to the dish.

Tiffany collapsed on the sofa with a sigh. She heard a click. Then the hotel suite door opened to reveal Randy. He took in the sight of her tangled hair, oversized shirt, and lack of pants with an amused smirk. "So we're both spending a lazy Sunday inside?"

Tiffany sat up. "Actually, I wanted to talk to Anna again. Caitlyn saw a couple elementalists yesterday on Fremont Street. Well, I'm assuming they're both elementalists. She saw the older one busking to feed the younger one, his little sister, we're guessing."

"Unsurprising," Randy said. "Your world has always had its share of visitors, and their world is another giant asteroid or two away from obliteration. I doubt they came with Brendon's henchmen only to end up in Vegas."

"Probably not," Tiffany agreed, "but Caitlyn wants to help them."

"I think Anna's spread a little thin as it is, but I can stay up a little longer if you want to talk to her this morning," Randy said. He sat beside Tiffany on the couch, giving one of her bare knees a squeeze.

"I kind of wanted to talk to her by myself," Tiffay said, rising. "Not just about the elementalists—other stuff. Girl stuff," she lied.

Randy raised his eyebrows but didn't pry. "Sure. You don't need me for the code."

"Thank you." Tiffany leaned forward to kiss him on the cheek. "Go get some rest."

"Tiffany," Anna said, welcoming her into the office. "I hope you're not here on business. I'm feeling a little burned out." Unlike Tiffany, who had changed out of her sleep shirt into a tank top and yoga pants, Anna still wore crimson silk pajamas, her dark curls escaping a loose braid held back with a velvet scrunchie.

"Not exactly," Tiffany said, sitting down in a chair across from Anna's desk.

"Good. Pretending to be Morgan can be such a chore." Anna sat back in her leather chair and propped her feet on the desk. "At least I figured out a way to make her stuffy business attire my own. Being based in Vegas makes me feel like I can play a little more with my sartorial choices. The real Morgan never let herself have any fun."

"You don't have to pretend with me," Tiffany said. "Not anymore. But aren't you worried about your sister?"

"A little," Anna said, "but if something truly dire happened to her, I think I'd be able to sense it. No, she's laying low for some reason. Just wish she'd keep someone else in the loop. I'm not sure how much longer I can stand to keep up the charade. I grow weary of this world."

Tiffany cut to the chase. "The other world, the one where you took the kids you rescued—do you think it could be a safe haven for other beings?"

"What sort of beings?" Anna slid her legs off the table and leaned forward.

"One of my dancers saw a young man busking on Fremont Street," Tiffany said. "An elementalist. She followed him to an alley and saw him feed a little girl—his sister, maybe. We're worried they might be homeless refugees."

"I suppose we shouldn't assume all elementalists mean us harm," Anna said slowly.

Tiffany felt a twinge of hope as Anna appeared to consider.

"But it's not really up to me."

Tiffany's heart sank.

"I may be Queen of the Underworld back home, but there I'm just one of seven on a council of elders. The eldest elder, by far, but I'm not going to pull rank," Anna said. "I can send word for my liaison between this world and the next, and he can pass along your information to the rest of the council. It's worth considering. Anything else?"

"I also heard there's a chance Emerson Fowler might get released from prison on a technicality," Tiffany said.

"Yes, I've seen the news. Well, the headlines anyway," She wrinkled her nose in distaste. "Lance worries Emerson might come for the Lafayette Foundation again, but I think he'd be wise to keep a low profile." Anna rose to her feet. "If that's all, I think I'll be returning to my bedchamber. I need to catch up on the latest episode of *Love in Paradise*. For some strange reason, I can't get enough of humans showing their asses. Metaphorically speaking, of course. They blur everything on network television."

"Actually," Tiffany said, "there is one more thing I wanted to talk to you about."

Anna sighed. "Is it about your show? We've secured the license for the use of live animals, and the wrangler is confirmed for next week."

"My cat started talking to me," Tiffany said.

Anna tilted her head, appearing confused. "I didn't know you were having a fight."

"What? No," Tiffany said. "I mean we can communicate now. With each other. We could never do that before," she added for further clarification.

Anna looked bored. "So, what's the problem?"

"I guess there isn't one," Tiffany said, flustered. "I was just worried I'm losing my mind. Also..." She paused as she considered her next words. "He's not very nice," she finished, painfully aware of how pathetic she must sound.

"If it's a hype man you wanted, you should have gotten a dog," Anna said. "Though I suppose you do have Randy." A wicked grin spread across her face as she sat back down. "I have to know, is it the man you're attracted to—or the wolf?"

Tiffany felt her cheeks warm. "That's a rather personal question."

"Oh, c'mon," Anna pleaded. "Do you know how long it's been since I've heard any decent gossip? I miss my human besties. It's nothing but business and political intrigue these days, minus the intrigue. Even the criminal conspiracies are boring. All those smarmy mafiosos angling to be the next Al Capone. Yawn."

"You're pretending to be one sister while the other broods somewhere, presumably plotting revenge for the death of her only son," Tiffany reminded her. "If anything, your present circumstances are a little too interesting for my personal comfort level."

"I may have gotten on the bad side of one of those mafiosos, too." Anna cringed as though she'd committed some minor faux pas and not the sort of offense that might lead to dismembered animal parts in her bed. "I thought running a casino would be fun, but it's just as bad as attending to Morgan's political matters. Maybe even worse."

Not knowing what else to say, Tiffany stood. "I don't want to take up any more of your time," she said. "Especially when you're dealing with so many problems already. Thank you so much for talking to me."

"Any time," Anna said. "Especially if you ever have any dirt to share… unless it means more work for me." She giggled. "I just want to hear the tea. I don't want to clean it up."

chapter ten

Caitlyn sat at a white wrought iron table in the Bluebelle Bakery. She picked a piece of caramelized bacon off her maple crème filled donut and chewed in quiet contemplation. Should she investigate the most recent murder down the block from Avalon, or join Amber, Emi, and Jade by the pool?

Memories of the angry manager and aerial gymnast from yesterday haunted Caitlyn, their flashing eyes and snarling mouths taking turns to condemn her. And she hadn't even learned anything useful. Not unless the mystery kid was the killer, but why slit someone's throat when you had the power to make them spontaneously combust?

Pool it is, Caitlyn decided. Her brain hurt from thinking.

Amber, Emi, and Jade were already stretched out on lounge chairs under umbrellas when Caitlyn met them down by the Enchanted Waters of Avalon. She stepped out of her sandals. Then she removed the pair of shorts she wore over her purple one-piece and set them on the fourth chair of their private shared cabana.

Not content to lay around doing nothing, Caitlyn jumped on the first available innertube she could find to float along the lazy river. She squealed with delight as she passed under the statue of a water nymph tipping a watering can. The cool water provided welcome relief from the hot July sun. The lazy river also drifted through dark breezy caverns and under waterfalls. Caitlyn knew the water was lit with changing LEDs at night, but even during the day, the experience felt as magical as the name implied—and so unlike the world Morgan and her kind had left behind.

Perhaps the world of the Fae was this beautiful once, but their sun had become a white dwarf. That's why they were nearly translucent behind their illusions, appearing almost blue. She heard their eyes were as black and fathomless as a shark's, probably due to their enlarged pupils attempting to capture as much dimming sunlight as possible. Caitlyn shivered despite the heat as she contemplated the reality of the Fae and their dying world.

Naturally, they were drawn to the vibrant sun and warmth of this world, though it was growing too warm for the comfort level of anyone not in denial. In her darkest moments, Caitlyn wondered if those who came here—Fae and elementalists alike—hadn't traded one dying world for another.

A boisterous teenager interrupted Caitlyn's unhappy thoughts when he tipped over her innertube. "Hey!" She lowered her sunglasses to glare at the offending boy. Caitlyn shrugged off his apologetic parents as she headed toward the steps out of the lazy river, but one of the lifeguards on duty had some choice words. The dangers of roughhousing aside, Caitlyn didn't care about keeping her messy haphazard half-bun dry. Her next stop was the waterslides.

Emi caught up to Caitlyn in line as she approached a set of three waterslides promising a mostly dark experience through winding caverns. "So where were you all day, anyway?"

"Just experiencing Fremont Street in all its touristy glory," Caitlyn said. "I thought I'd explore my career options for when the Vegas residency ends," she joked with a wry grin. "Then I saw Fire and Ash was playing the main stage, so I let Tiffany know. We met up and hung out with the band after the show."

"Boo," Emi said. "I'm always up for Fremont Street."

"Sorry," Caitlyn said. "It was all very spur of the moment." And as much business as pleasure, she realized. Emi and the others were largely insulated from all the intergalactic drama, except for when Tiffany being outed as part-Fae temporarily derailed the tour.

"Race you to the bottom," Emi said when it was their turn to slide.

· · ·

After riding a few slides, Caitlyn ordered a hibiscus lemonade slush—complete with a pretty red tropical flower—at the snack bar. She stretched out on her lounge chair to dry while Amber, Emi, and Jade debated dinner plans. "I can't believe I'm saying this," she told them, "but I think I need a quiet night in. Yesterday was a long day, and this week will be crazy busy."

"Now that you mention it," Jade said, "I don't take advantage of our room service discount as often as I should."

"We can catch up on *Love in Paradise*," Amber said.

"Ugh" Emi chimed in. "Shawna is the worst."

"So smug," Jade agreed.

Caitlyn closed her eyes and drifted off while the other women talked about people she didn't know and wouldn't care to know. When she awoke, they had gone.

You looked so peaceful, read a note left on her chair. *We didn't want to wake you.*

Too bad they didn't close the drapes before leaving, Caitlyn thought. The sun had moved, and with it, some of the shade. Her right arm and shoulder prickled painfully, but she supposed she shared in the blame for failing to reapply sunblock before her nap.

Groaning, Caitlyn sat up and swung her legs over the lounge chair to leave.

"Ooh," said a passing cocktail waitress. She wore a bikini top and miniskirt covered in fake leaves and pink flowers, her brown hair braided and entwined with more leaves and flowers. "You should get some aloe on that. I think they carry some in the marketplace."

"Ouch," said the clerk. "That looks like it hurts."

"Hence the aloe vera," Caitlyn told her, hoping she didn't sound bitchy as she set the bottle down on the counter. The clerk appeared unoffended as she rang up the order, which also included a pint of ice cream and some potato chips.

Caitlyn left the marketplace and almost walked right into Nick, of all people. He wore a dark green v-neck, which annoyingly enhanced his eyes, and chinos.

"Oh, hey, Daphne," he said, after glancing at her purple swimsuit a split second too long. "Picking up Scooby snacks?"

"Something like that," Caitlyn said. "Why are you here?"

"After seeing you yesterday, I realized I haven't been to Avalon yet," Nick said. "I have the day off so I thought I'd check out the 'Disneyfied abomination that belies the existential threat the Fae menace poses humanity.'"

Caitlyn raised an eyebrow. Did Nick even know what "existential" meant?

"My roommate watches too much TV news," Nick explained. "The reporters and their guests get a little hyper about Morgan le Fay. I guess I shouldn't blame them after what happened in New York City, but this place seems nice. And nobody's tried to knock you upside the head as far as I can tell, so it's already an improvement over past experience." He grinned.

"That's very fair of you," Caitlyn said.

"I'm nothing if not open-minded." Nick's smile widened.

"Okay," Caitlyn said. "I should get going before my ice cream melts." She was beginning to feel a little out of sorts. Maybe because of the sunburn.

"Sure," Nick said, "but if you get bored and want something more substantial to eat, I might hit up the steakhouse later. Depends on how well I do on the floor. I made so many tips last night during the concert. Thought I'd try my luck at blackjack. Same number?"

Caitlyn nodded despite her discomfort. The prickly warmth had spread from her sunburn to the rest of her body. She wondered if her face was blotchy and—oh, no—she'd forgotten about the wild half-wet tangles hanging down her back. Certain she looked like a hot mess, Caitlyn was beginning to suspect Nick was having fun at her expense, but she forced herself to maintain a neutral expression as he talked.

"Doubt you saved mine, but I can text you. Lemme know if you want to meet up for dinner. I'll place a reservation for two just in case." Nick looked almost shy as he added, "It's been a while since I've seen a friendly...well, a familiar face anyway."

～

Five minutes later, Caitlyn put her ice cream in the freezer, then collapsed on the sofa. She realized she hadn't heard any notifications on her phone. Caitlyn pulled it out of the pocket of her shorts to reaffirm that Nick hadn't sent a text after all. Instead of relief, she felt an unexpected twinge of disappointment.

"Be less dumb," she told herself.

What did Caitlyn care about Nick teasing her anyway?

The guy had cheated on his ex with her best friend after a director abducted the poor woman to feed to his psychic vampire muse. Of course, Nick hadn't known about any of that. Not until after Caitlyn helped rescue his ex. And was Caitlyn any better, hanging on Nick less than a week after breaking up with someone else?

"Ugh!"

Caitlyn pushed herself off the sofa and walked into the bathroom. She turned on the shower so she could rinse the chlorine off her skin and out of her hair. Wincing as the water hit her sunburn, Caitlyn reached for shampoo. She tried to push Nick out of her brain while she scrubbed her scalp, then conditioned her hair.

The murderer. That was what she needed to think about, Caitlyn reminded herself as she dried off. She picked up her phone to see if there were any new updates on the case.

Instead, she saw a message from Nick:

Wild Hunt confirmed the reservation for six. Hope to see you there.

"Oh, come on!"

Caitlyn threw her phone into the next room, where it bounced harmlessly on the king bed.

chapter eleven

The hostess led Caitlyn up the stairs to a table overlooking the restaurant. She felt something she hadn't felt in a long time, even on stage. Hell, even during yesterday's disastrous investigation attempt on Fremont Street. Nervous, Caitlyn remembered. That's what that icky tingly feeling was.

"Starling, I wasn't sure if you'd actually come." Nick grinned as Caitlyn sat across from him with a nervous smile of her own.

"Yeah, well, after you mentioned Wild Hunt, I thought about how good a burger sounded," Caitlyn said. "And I figured it might be kind of rude to come eat by myself, so…here I am," she finished lamely. "Are you gonna keep calling me detective names?"

"Maybe," Nick said. "Nice dress."

Caitlyn hadn't wanted to wear a dress, but she didn't want to wear anything that brushed against her sunburn either. A tank top felt too casual for a nice steakhouse, so she'd settled on a tropical print dress with spaghetti straps. If Nick noticed the sunburn, he kept it to himself.

"How did blackjack go?"

Nick looked pleased with himself. "Dinner's on me," he said. "Order whatever you want. The ribeye for two sounds good."

Caitlyn wanted to protest, but then she remembered how messy the burger could be. She decided she'd have a much easier time pretending to be civilized with a knife and fork. Nick ordered a bottle of wine, too. Not just a glass, the whole bottle. This was starting to feel a lot like...well, a date. *What did you expect it to be?* Caitlyn asked herself as she spread sea-salted butter onto a slice of fresh sourdough bread.

"You still look unsure about being here," Nick observed with irritating accuracy. "I know I didn't have the best reputation during *Dracula*, but I was going through kind of a tough time. I didn't handle things as well as I probably should've."

Caitlyn set her bread down before taking a bite. "You cheated on your girlfriend with her best friend."

Nick looked annoyed but unsurprised. "She broke up with me before she disappeared," he said. "Told me she met someone better who could make all her dreams come true. I figured she ran off with a Moroccan prince to become the next Grace Kelly or something. How was I supposed to know she meant that dweeb Elliot?"

"Fair point," Caitlyn acquiesced, "but what about her friend?"

"What about her?" Nick shrugged. "We kissed maybe once or twice. Mostly she just complained about Anne Marie. Kinda felt used, to be honest. It was embarrassing. Not failed-actor-slinging-drinks-in-Vegas embarrassing, but it's up there." He smirked, an unruly tendril of dark hair falling onto his forehead.

Caitlyn bit her lip on a smile. "I may have misjudged you," she said after a beat. "I'm sorry." She finished buttering her bread and took a bite to avoid making eye contact. "Did you ever talk to Anne Marie after what happened?"

"Once." Nick's smile faded. "She was..." He paused as he appeared to search for the right words. "Nice, I guess, but distant. Like we had never dated. She didn't seem to remember much, but I don't know if any of it was for real or just an act to save face. I heard she's getting back into performing, though. Mostly off-off-Broadway. What about you?"

"Still performing, obviously."

"Yeah, but backup to Tiffany Sharp?" Nick's brow furrowed. "Seems beneath you."

Caitlyn frowned. "I've learned a lot about show business the past few years. Mostly I learned that I like to perform, but I also value my privacy. I don't have to be the center of attention to enjoy myself. I prefer it this way."

Nick looked unconvinced, but a server appeared with their entrees. While they ate, Caitlyn learned Nick was saving money to move to Los Angeles and reignite his career on screen instead of the stage. His parents had cut him off after the *Dracula* musical fell through, and he refused to take part in the family business like his siblings had. His family owned a small regional chain of diners back east. As an only child, Caitlyn could not relate to his plight as the middle of three children, but she nodded sympathetically as he complained about the uptight brother he'd failed to emulate and the spoiled sister who got everything she wanted.

"I'm sorry," Nick said after the server cleared their plates. "I feel like I've been monopolizing the conversation."

"That's okay," Caitlyn said. "I like to listen."

"I feel like everything I know about you I've learned from the tabloids," Nick said. "Not on purpose," he added quickly. "You'd basically have to live under a rock to avoid seeing or hearing anything about Tiffany and her inner circle."

Caitlyn shrugged. "What you see is what you get."

"C'mon, you know all my family drama." Nick leaned forward. "What's your story?"

Caitlyn pressed her lips together. She wasn't sure why she didn't want to talk about her family. Maybe because less than a day ago they were trading insults. She wasn't ready to talk about her mom, and she didn't want Nick's pity. The server returned with a dessert menu before Caitlyn could think of a reply.

"The seven-layer chocolate cake sounds good," Nick said.

It did, but Caitlyn was even less ready to share cake than she was to divulge personal details. "No thanks," she said. "I have to be up early for rehearsal. I should really call it a night. Thank you for dinner. And the company."

Nick looked disappointed but declined dessert and asked for the check.

Caitlyn rose to her feet.

Nick stood as well. He took a step toward her, then hesitated before holding out his hand. Instead of a handshake, he lifted her hand to his lips. "Maybe next time," he said.

Caitlyn felt too surprised to say anything. Instead, she nodded and walked away, stifling a yelp when her thigh caught the corner of the next table. That was going to leave a mark.

Caitlyn groaned when her alarm went off the next morning. The last thing she remembered before drifting off to sleep was replaying her date with Nick, trying to figure out if she'd said or did something wrong, and what, if anything, she should make of the kiss.

It was just your hand. It didn't mean anything.

But what if it did?

It didn't!

Caitlyn forced herself out of bed to get ready before the irritating debate raged anew. She hoped rehearsal would provide a welcome distraction for her busy brain.

"Rough night?" Amber asked as Caitlyn walked into the dressing room.

Caitlyn looked at her reflection in the mirror. Apart from faint shadows under her eyes, she looked more or less the same. She considered mentioning her date with Nick, but decided she didn't want to face a barrage of questions from Amber, Emi, and Jade.

Well, maybe not Jade. The dancer appeared uninterested as she looked in the mirror to apply lip gloss.

"I don't think any of us are sleeping well now that the Fremont Street Killer is expanding his territory," Emi said, rescuing Caitlyn from Amber's searching gaze. She pulled her straight black hair into a ponytail.

"I'm not worried," Jade said. "If an all-powerful fairy queen like Morgan le Fay can't keep us safe, nobody can."

Emi frowned, considering. "That's not really as comforting as I think you mean it to be."

"No, I agree with Jade," Amber said. "But that's why it's important to stick together. Speaking of which." Her attention returned to Caitlyn. "Where were you last night? Wouldn't hurt to keep each other informed in case anything happens."

"I never left the hotel," Caitlyn answered. "We should start warming up."

Amber narrowed her eyes but didn't pry.

"The Vegas Ripper. That's what they're calling him now," Caitlyn overheard a stagehand say into a headset when she walked backstage. Other stagehands milled around, organizing the prop table or moving rolling set pieces onto the stage for the first act of Tiffany's production.

"Did he get someone else?" Emi squeezed past Caitlyn to ask the stagehand.

He was tall and lanky, and stood with his hands shoved into the pockets of his cargo shorts. Like the other stagehands, he wore a nondescript black tee simply labeled Crew. He removed one of his hands from his pockets to nervously run his fingers through sandy hair. "A trapeze artist that works—well, worked—at our next-door neighbor's. They found her body in a stairwell leading to the parking garage."

Emi covered her mouth, eyes wide.

"Sorry," the stagehand said, looking anxious. "Was that TMI?"

"Bet someone from here's gonna be next," said another stagehand as she walked up to him. She wore paint-speckled overalls, the pockets holding paint brushes of different sizes. Dark hair fell into one of her eyes, but the other appeared to glitter with gleeful malevolence.

"Not cool, Becky," said the first stagehand. "Don't you have a flat to finish painting?"

"Whatever."

"She seems nice," Amber said, stepping beside Caitlyn.

The first stagehand gave Amber a look of apology. "I gotta finish setting up the stage," he told them after clearing his throat. "Everyone's sitting in the audience to wait for Tiffany."

After exchanging uneasy glances with Amber, Emi, and Jade, Caitlyn walked with them down the side of the stage. They dodged more stagehands and set pieces until they reached the stairs leading out into the audience. Most of the other performers were already sitting, talking amongst themselves in low uneasy voices.

A somber Tiffany walked on stage shortly after Caitlyn sat down, and a stagehand affixed a mic to the strap of her pink tank top. "Mic check, one, two," Tiffany said, her voice clear as a bell. She nodded at someone behind

Caitlyn, probably the sound technician in the sound booth. "So, by now I'm sure everyone heard about the latest killing. Morgan le Fay wanted me to reaffirm her commitment to your safety and to remind you about using the buddy system whenever possible."

Unhappy murmurs spread throughout the audience.

Tiffany looked down at the stage before continuing to speak. When she looked back up, her eyes appeared to glisten. A couple tears traced trails down her cheeks. "I probably should have done this before, but I'd like us to bow our heads for a moment of silence to recognize last night's victim. All the victims, really."

Emi took Caitlyn's hand. The silence was broken only by the occasional sniffle.

"Okay," Tiffany said after a minute or two. "Let's get to work. The animal wrangler arrives after lunch, so I want to get through the first act in its entirety at least once. There may be some hiccups as we get used to working with the set, but the major changes happen between acts."

People rose to their feet. Caitlyn hung back to wait. She noticed a dancer hunched over in her chair, trembling. She remembered her name was Sara. Caitlyn walked to her and sat down. "Did you know the victim?" she asked softly, inwardly cursing herself for saying "victim" instead of the name. It sounded so cold and impersonal.

The red-haired dancer looked up at Caitlyn with a blotchy tear-stained face. "Melanie was my cousin," Sara said. "She auditioned for this show, too, but she didn't make the cut."

"I'm so sorry," Caitlyn said. "I can talk to Tiffany if you need more time. I'm sure she'd understand."

"No," Sara said, wiping away her tears. "I'll be okay. But thanks." She stood.

Caitlyn took a deep shaky breath and followed. She looked at the stage. Tiffany met her eyes, raising her brows in a question. Caitlyn gave her a thumbs-up. Tiffany nodded. *The show must go on,* her look said. Caitlyn shivered.

Déjà vu.

Caitlyn found herself staring up at the rafters as she walked to the stage. No glowing eyes in the shadows. No sketchy sounds below or offstage, either. Just the muted conversations of cast and crew, even the occasional giggle before the opening swell of music announcing the prelude of the show. Dancers took their places on and off the stage. For Caitlyn, Amber, Emi, and Jade, that meant flanking broken columns on either side to await Tiffany's entrance.

Caitlyn took a few more deep breaths to steady herself. As Tiffany sang the opening of the song "Legendary" that had launched her career, the women left their pillars to join her center stage, and Caitlyn lost herself in the music. While she knew Tiffany now cringed inwardly at lyrics like "I'm going to be so legendary. Just you wait and see. So legendary. Nobody's gonna stop me," the song had a driving bass line and remained a fan favorite.

The overarching concept of the show was transformation, with a tongue-in-cheek nod at Tiffany's otherworldly origin, but each act was themed around the stages of a magic trick. The first act would present the audience with something ordinary, in this case Tiffany as a regular girl. It closed with "Stranger to Myself," hinting at the transformation to come.

Dancers left the stage as Tiffany's piano appeared from a rising platform beneath a trapdoor. Caitlyn loved to watch from offstage. No prerecorded backing track. No special effects, apart from a gentle mist lit in soft pink and blue light that enveloped the stage like a cloud. Just Tiffany and her piano.

Tiffany's voice cracked with emotion on the last line of the song, but the cast and crew burst into applause. She stood and gave a bashful little bow, so different from the swagger and bravado she had to project during "Legendary" at the top of the act.

Caitlyn beamed, but her smile faded when she heard a flurry of movement in the rafters.

"I warned you about placing gels too close to the light," she overheard Joe saying into his headset. The stage manager was a slight man with a receding hairline, but competent and commanding.

Caitlyn relaxed.

No monsters, only a minor tech mishap.

"Pizza in the green room," Joe yelled, moving the mic on his headset away from his mouth.

He didn't have to tell Caitlyn twice.

chapter twelve

Tiffany slipped into her dressing room with a single slice of pizza and a small salad. She felt weird about rehearsing while a murder investigation took place in the neighboring hotel, especially when some of the cast and crew knew the latest victim.

Someone knocked on the door. "Can I come in?" Caitlyn asked.

"Of course."

Caitlyn came in and sat on the floor, holding a paper plate loaded with pizza in her lap. "I couldn't decide if I wanted cheese, pepperoni, or supreme, so I got one of everything. Jade asked how I could eat so much at a time like this, but we danced our asses off out there." She looked at Tiffany, her eyes wide with apparent concern. "Does it make me a bad person if death doesn't spoil my appetite?"

"No," Tiffany told her. "I'm pretty sure it just makes you hungry. We all handle death differently. I wasn't sure if I should call off rehearsal altogether, but I'm not sure if wallowing in fear or misery would do anyone any favors, so I'm leaving it up to the cast and crew to decide for themselves. Probably ending rehearsal early whatever day there's a wake, though."

"I think everyone's safest when we're all together here at the Avalon," Caitlyn said between bites of pizza. "I probably shouldn't say anything, but I ran into an old friend the other day. I'm surprised he hasn't caught the killer already, but I feel safer knowing he's around."

One of Morgan le Fay's agents, Tiffany presumed. She'd seen or sensed a few herself, but nobody else seemed to notice when a slice of pizza had floated away earlier. "Randy's been pulling all-nighters, too," she said. "To patrol."

"Bummer for you," Caitlyn said, "but you do seem better rested than you have in a while." She grinned.

Tiffany felt her cheeks warm. "I've been having a lot of bad dreams lately!"

"You don't have to explain yourself," Caitlyn said. "I don't think I'd be able to get a lot of sleep with a guy like Randy around." She sighed. "I can't even remember the last time I, uh, didn't get a lot of sleep."

"Probably not the best time to meet someone new," Tiffany said slowly.

"Oh, please!" Caitlyn scoffed. "Like I would ever get romantically involved with some fiendish Fae felon—no offense. I'm, like, a total bloodhound at detecting otherworldly beings. I mean, you and Brendan may not have registered on my fae-dar, but you're only half, and I did know *something* was off about that guy."

"Okay, okay," Tiffany laughed. "Knock yourself out."

Caitlyn blanched. "I think I ate too much."

Tiffany watched her leave, concerned. She decided to extend lunch another half hour.

The animal wrangler was late, anyway.

"So sorry," a breathless Yasmin Costa said, tucking a loose strand of black hair behind her ear. "Traffic was a total nightmare once we reached the city. I thought L.A. drivers were crazy, but Vegas drivers might be worse."

A couple of assistant wranglers in matching Animal All-Stars tees stood behind Yasmin, carrying a large terrarium covered with a sheet. They would care for the snake during the beginning of Tiffany's residency, complete with room and board, until they trained their replacements for the duration.

Tiffany had worked with Yasmin's Animal All-Stars company before. The first time, she used a Chilean rose tarantula in her "Under Your Spell" video. Now Tiffany was incorporating a Burmese python into the second act of her show as an homage to one of her favorite artists growing up, only this python would be the usual brown and black instead of yellow.

"I'll show you to the snake's, uh, dressing room," the stage manager, Joe, said. "At least it's not tigers," he muttered under his breath. In a louder voice, Joe asked Yasmin, "He doesn't bite, does he?"

"Pythons are constrictors." Yasmin grinned at Joe. "He's a hugger." To Tiffany, she said, "Perhaps we should do introductions in the dressing room first. That way you can get a good sense of his weight and movement before we bring Perry on stage. Do you know which dancers will assist you?"

Tiffany stifled a giggle at the snake's name. "Sure," she said. "Justin, Miguel, join us!" she called to a couple muscular dancers undaunted by the prospect of handling a snake.

"Are your hands always thisss cold?"

Tiffany stiffened.

"Relax," Yasmin said. "Perry can sense when you're nervous."

"Sorry," Tiffany said. "He's just a little heavier than I expected. I might need to up my weights during my next workout." She stood just outside a large dressing room modified for her "special guest performer," as the sign outside the door said.

Perry traveled in a modest terrarium, but required an enclosure that was ten feet long by six feet wide by six feet tall. A freezer for the snake's food encompassed another good chunk of real estate.

After Perry's unexpected commentary, Tiffany shuddered at the thought of live food. One of Yasmin's assistants, her cousin Davi, had gone back out to the company van to retrieve a cooler to stock the fridge. The other assistant, Jenna, a short but strong woman with a multicolored pixie cut and pale freckled skin, made sure the UV lights and heat lamps for the enclosure were working properly.

Tiffany felt a twinge of guilt. She hadn't realized how big of an undertaking she had requested, but "Morgan le Fay" hadn't even batted an eye at the expense or Perry's housing demands. Tiffany supposed money remained as foreign a concept to Anna as tact and decorum, or perhaps the Lafayette Corporation was just that loaded.

Miguel and Justin took turns holding Perry, then wrapping him around Tiffany's shoulders. Davi returned with the cooler. Tiffany averted her eyes while he transferred food into the freezer. "The second act of my show opens with 'Under Your Spell,'" Tiffany told Yasmin. "Next is 'Go Wild.' Then, I segue into 'Free 2 Dance' with an interpolation of an old favorite. Miguel or Justin will give me Perry at the beginning, then take him away before the chorus."

Jenna poked her head out of Perry's enclosure. "You're doing all this for one song?" She let out a low whistle.

"And we're thrilled to be a part of it," Yasmin said with a pointed glare at Jenna. She turned back to Tiffany with a wide smile. "Sounds fabulous. Let's make it happen."

After Tiffany sang and danced through a clean run of "Under Your Spell" and "Go Wild", she waited for Miguel and Justine to drape Perry over her shoulders as the music transitioned into "Free 2 Dance." As the snake settled into position, Tiffany spun around the part of the stage where the drummer would sit for the live show as the audio track played over the speakers. She had grown used to the feel of the smooth, muscular snake around her neck and shoulders, but not the satiny hiss of his voice.

"Ssso much better," Perry whispered, his tongue tickling Tiffany's earlobe. "I don't feel like I'm being handled by a corpse."

"Not the time," Tiffany hissed back, grateful for the backing track.

Caitlyn, who was reclining nearby on a lyra suspended over the stage, gave her a strange look before gracefully dismounting. Tiffany played it off as she turned to give Perry back to Miguel before wrapping herself around Justin's broad chest. Nobody else appeared to have noticed anything. The rest of the second act continued without a hitch.

After a short snack break, the cast and crew ran through the third act. Tiffany waited until everyone had gone for the night before slipping into Perry's room using a master key entrusted to a select few. Randy had one, too. So did Anna, of course.

"So." Tiffany peered into the shadowy habitat. The only source of light streamed under the door from the hallway. "I can understand snakes, too."

"Wish I could understand ratsss," Perry hissed from somewhere in the darkness.

"They're frozen." Tiffany made a face.

"Not those ratsss. The ratsss in the walls. They're agitated about sssomething."

"There's no rats in the walls," Tiffany said. "Avalon is a very clean hotel." She felt silly defending her temporary home to a snake, but then, talking to a snake at all was pretty silly—albeit even more unnerving than her conversations with Groucho Manx.

"All walls have ratsss in them."

Tiffany shivered. Her eyes having adjusted to the dark, she could just make out Perry's black eyes peering at her from a tall branch in his enclosure.

"Find the ratsss."

chapter thirteen

F ind the ratsss.

Perry's sinister hiss repeated in Tiffany's brain on a loop while she tried to enjoy a quiet dinner in her suite with Randy before his shift. She felt her boyfriend's eyes on her as she twirled pasta around her fork without lifting it to her lips.

"Something wrong?" Randy asked.

"Have you ever seen any rats in Avalon?" Tiffany asked, trying to sound casual.

"Once or twice," Randy said. "Usually in the stairwells or the back alleyways. And never in the kitchens. Why?"

"I thought I heard something skittering around backstage during rehearsal," Tiffany lied. "Hope they don't chew wires."

"Maintenance is pretty good about removing rats," Randy said. "Humanely," he was quick to add. "Anna has sort of a soft spot for creepy crawlies and other things that go bump in the night. Probably a holdover from living in the Underworld."

"I hope that soft spot doesn't extend to reavers," Tiffany said.

"Nope," Randy said. "I think Vegas is too hot and dry for them. Not that many lurking in California, either. The biggest infestations have all been on the east coast."

"Infestations," Tiffany repeated. "There's so many reavers on the east coast, they qualify as infestations. How nice." She set her fork down and pushed her plate away. "Don't think I have the appetite for dessert."

Randy reached out to squeeze her shoulder. "Try to relax," he said. "Maybe take a bubble bath. I'll box up our leftovers before I leave for work."

Tiffany decided to take Randy's advice after he left for the night. She dimmed the lights, then filled the large whirlpool tub in the bathroom with hot water and lavender vanilla-scented bubbles while she undressed. After she sank into the tub, Tiffany reached for a washcloth to cover her face. Soft music played from a stereo built into the bathroom wall.

"You've been hearing them, too, huh?"

Tiffany bolted upright, the washcloth falling into the sudsy water with a splash. Groucho Manx stared at her from the white and gold marble bathroom counter.

"Hearing who?" Tiffany asked warily despite knowing the answer.

"The rats," Groucho Manx said. "They try to keep their voices low even though Gizmo's never gonna catch 'em, but we still hear them chattering to each other. Usually, it's nothing important. What their favorite snacks are, where to find them, how to evade the no-kill traps that maintenance leaves around…"

Tiffany raised a hand out of the water and twirled her finger as if Groucho Manx could even interpret her "get to the point" gesture. He must have sensed her impatience because he continued, "Sometimes they talk about what's under the hotel, and who's been lurking around it. Not just Wolf Boy and the Fae in the black suits, someone new." His pupils grew wider.

"The only thing under the hotel is ten feet of ceme…wait, what do you mean, someone new?" Tiffany shivered despite the hot water that maintained its temperature. She hugged her legs to her chest and rested her chin on her knees.

"Someone—some*thing*—came slinking around the hotel last night. He never came in, but he stank of blood and death and malevolence," Groucho Manx said ominously. Tiffany found herself missing his usual biting sarcasm.

"Malevolence?" she asked, surprised. "Those were their exact words?"

"I'm not exactly fluent in 'rat,' but that was the general idea," Groucho Manx said. "Did I mention it was fresh blood? *Human* blood."

Tiffany felt her eyes widen as she realized the implication. "He must have come here after he killed that poor girl." She rose from the tub and reached for a fluffy white towel to wrap around herself. "But why?"

"Hungry for more?" Groucho Manx suggested. "How should I know? I'm just a housecat."

"He's probably already scouting for his next kill," Tiffany said to herself. "Randy will get him," she decided. "I'm sure of it."

"Didn't get him last night," Groucho muttered under his breath.

Tiffany's grip on her towel tightened.

chapter fourteen

" I need to see Anna again," Tiffany told Randy the next morning. She stood in the living room, already dressed in a tank top and bike shorts for rehearsal. "I...I think the killer was outside Avalon the night he killed Melanie."

"I did find blood in the alley," Randy said, "but I can't confirm it's Melanie's. Why do you think he was here? Just a hunch?"

"Not exactly," Tiffany said. *Might as well rip the metaphorical bandage off,* she thought before saying, "Groucho Manx said the rats sensed him in the alley that very same night." She braced herself for Randy's response. He stared at her for what felt like an eternity, then sat down on the sofa.

"So, you can understand Groucho Manx, and he, apparently, can understand rats." Now Randy appeared to be lost in thought, probably debating whether to dump Tiffany, have her institutionalized, or both.

"It sounds crazy, I know," Tiffany said. Groucho Manx emerged from behind the sofa.

"No, no," Randy said, "I've always suspected some animals had psychic ability, maybe even people, though not so much the frauds I've encountered here. And like we talked about the other day, it serves an obvious evolutionary advantage—to predator and prey alike."

"I don't eat rodents like some sort of...*savage*," Groucho Manx scoffed. "You know I prefer fine dining in a can."

"What I don't understand is why you danced around telling me about your own ability," Randy continued, oblivious to the disgruntled feline. "It's not like we didn't expect latent fae abilities to emerge now that you knew who you really are. Didn't you trust me?"

"I doubt even Gizmo would know what to do with one if he caught it." Groucho Manx hopped into the chair beside the sofa. "He just wants to play."

Tiffany felt a headache developing as she tried to tune out his ranting to focus on Randy. She sat beside her boyfriend on the sofa. "I was afraid you wouldn't believe me. I didn't believe it myself, but then Perry told me about the rats, and Groucho Manx corroborated his story, and I knew I couldn't keep the secret to myself any longer, not when lives are at stake."

Randy furrowed his brow. "Who's Perry?"

"So, we're relying on the secondhand testimony of a snake and a cat," Anna said when Tiffany and Randy met with her in her office. She wore black satin pajamas today.

"I don't think they're making it up," Tiffany said.

"Me neither," Anna said, "but that means Convict Two knows how much security we have. Maybe it scared him off."

"Security never saw him," Randy pointed out, "or even smelled him, in my case."

"Then we'll keep someone stationed at every possible entrance tonight," Anna said, looking pleased with herself. "And I'll have Lance watch all of the other night's security footage. Last night's, too, if there's a chance he came back and you missed him twice. In the meantime—she reached under her desk to grab something—"say hello to my new best friend!"

"Aw," Randy said, leaning forward. "He's just a little guy."

"Little?" Tiffany said. "My third-grade teacher had rats. He's at least twice their size."

"Please don't kill me," squeaked the large brown rat. "I have a family."

"I'm not going to kill you, silly." Anna gently stroked the rat's head. "I just have a few questions to ask."

"You understood him?" Tiffany didn't know why she was surprised.

"Of course," Anna said. "I lived alone in a cave for over a hundred years before Morgan found me. I was pretty much raised by soul eaters. I'd be lonely if I never learned to communicate with other beings. Though the closest critter our world has to rats is way less smart and sociable. But enough about me." She turned her attention back to the rat she still held in the palm of her hands. "Tell me about the bad man."

"It's just like the cat and the snake told you," said the rat in a calmer voice. "He was lurking in the alley. I was trying to eat some stale popcorn, but when he showed up, I ran away and hid under a cardboard box in a dark corner. I've encountered some bad things in my time—feral cats, rabid coyotes—but I never believed in evil before I smelled him."

"If you and any other members of your family would be willing to serve as scouts and alert me to his presence," Anna told the rat as she set him gently on the desk, "arrangements could be made for you to dine on something better than stale popcorn."

The rat stood on his hind legs. "It would be an honor, my lady."

Randy looked as dumbfounded as Tiffany felt. "So, that's a thing that just happened," she said after the rat hopped down to the floor.

"Did he accept your offer?" Randy asked Anna.

Anna grinned. "Apart from my distaste for business meetings and slimeballs in suits, I much prefer ruling this underworld to the one back home. What a charming little gentleman," she said, watching the rat scamper to a small hole in the wall Tiffany hadn't noticed before. "The fear suckers could never."

Tiffany rose to leave. "Oh, I almost forgot. Any news about the elementalist children?"

"I sent word to my liaison," Anna said, "but I'm still waiting to hear back. Do you want me to send someone to Fremont Street to check on them? Maybe throw some extra money in the boy's baseball cap?"

"Anything we can do to help," Tiffany told her. "If we gain their trust, maybe you can offer them a place to stay here." She didn't know how far she could push Anna's generosity with Morgan's money, but she wanted to plant the seed. "I hate the thought of them sleeping on the street, especially with a killer lurking around town."

"I'll think about it," Anna said. "We still don't know anything about them, but I'll see what I can find out." She rose to her feet, adding a note of finality to the meeting. "I suppose I should put some real clothes on and start my day. Byee!"

"What's a fear sucker?" Tiffany asked Randy after they returned to the suite.

"Something I wouldn't wanna say ten times fast in mixed company." Randy strode across the living room. "They're these rodent-sized nightmares that feed on fear. Nasty little critters," he said over his shoulder. "I've only encountered them once or twice."

Tiffany followed Randy into the bedroom as he disrobed. "When you say rodent-sized, do you mean like rats? Or capybaras?" she asked. "Because that feels like a crucial distinction."

"Rats," Randy said, climbing into bed. "But their small stature just makes it easier for them to sneak up on their victims. And they travel in packs." He must have seen Tiffany shudder in the dark, because Randy added, "I think that ill-fated production of the Dracula musical in New York City was the only known incursion into your world. Or maybe predators get to them before they can hurt anyone."

Tiffany watched as Randy clasped a pillow to his chest and rolled onto his side before dozing off. She envied the pillow and longed for a return to their normal routine.

chapter fifteen

"Are you okay?"

Startled, Caitlyn looked at Amber's reflection in the dressing room mirror. "I'm fine. Why do you ask?"

The dancer redid her long blond ponytail with a pink velvet scrunchie, avoiding Caitlyn's eyes. "I dunno, you've just been going through the motions all morning. And your grand pliés during 'Fairytale' looked a little—" Amber hesitated.

"Wonky?" Emi offered. She sat in the chair on the other side of Amber.

"It looked like you were laying an egg," Jade said, taking a seat at the far end.

Caitlyn felt too tired to take offense. "I couldn't sleep," she told them. "I just...I had this horrible thought. Like, what if the killer is one of the Fae?" Caitlyn knew she had to choose her words carefully, but she didn't want to leave her friends defenseless. "They can look like whoever they want, so how does anyone really know who's safe?"

Now the others looked around at each other, alarmed.

"I hate to say it," Jade said, "but Cat has a point."

"So, what do we do?" Amber turned to Caitlyn.

"I know!" Emi said, sounding excited. "Right now, we're all obviously who we say we are, even if Cat's a little off her game—no offense."

Caitlyn sighed. "None taken."

"We should come up with some sort of code for when we see each other outside rehearsal or need to buddy up," Emi continued. "Like a nonsense phrase only we know? But it has to be something easy to remember!"

"The cow flies home at midnight?" Jade smirked.

"Pretty sure it's 'crow.'" Amber giggled. "The *crow* flies home at midnight."

"Too basic," Emi said. "Besides, real code phrases should sound like normal speech. My great aunt was a secret agent for the NPA. How about something like this: one person says 'my muscles are sore' and the other one says 'try soaking in Epsom salt'?"

"But Emi," Amber said, "You and I just had that exact conversation last week."

"Exactly," Emi said. She gave Amber a triumphant smile. "And you remembered it!"

Jade rolled her eyes. "Now that we have that settled, do you really think the killer is one of the Fae?" she asked Caitlyn. "Usually, you're the first to defend them. Now you think one has it in for Vegas showgirls?"

"I'll defend the good ones like Morgan and Tiffany, if you think of her that way, sure," Caitlyn said. "But they have their fair share of baddies, too. I just want to make sure we've considered all the possibilities."

"You're the Fae expert," Jade grudgingly conceded.

Emi and Amber nodded in agreement.

After rehearsal, Caitlyn headed to the marketplace to restock soda. She was surprised to see Nick emerge from the nearby men's room. He looked more casual today, in a black tee and jeans, like he had come straight from work.

"I'm not stalking you, I swear." Nick held up his hands as he walked to Caitlyn. "Told Dan—he's my roommate—about my luck at blackjack, and he wanted to stop by after work." He looked down before saying in a softer voice, "I had a good time the other night." Nick looked back up and tried to meet Caitlyn's eyes, smiling a little.

"Right," Caitlyn said. She looked past him to peer at the casino floor. "So, where's Dan?"

Nick shrugged. "I think he moved on to roulette. Someone kept hitting when the dealer didn't have a ten showing and ruining it for the whole table. Hey, are you okay?" He reached out to put a hand on the side of Caitlyn's arm. "Is it because I haven't messaged you? I'm sorry. I didn't want to come on too strong."

A family walked by, giving them strange looks.

Caitlyn shrugged off Nick's hand. She ducked into a small alcove with chairs and small tables. "It's just weird the way I come here, dancers start dying, and then you show up all the way from New York City." She stared at the carpet, avoiding his eyes.

"I was here first," Nick sputtered. "I moved in with Dan well over a year ago. He's the one who helped me get the bartending gig. Let's go find him. You can ask him yourse—"Nick paused. "Wait a minute!" he said in a hushed voice. "Do you think *I* had something to do with those dancers? It's one thing to think I'm a crap boyfriend, but I'd never try to hurt anyone."

"Nick wouldn't," Caitlyn said. "But a faerie pretending to be Nick might."

Nick stared, incredulous. "Why would a faerie pretend to be me?"

"Maybe they saw us talking and decided they could use you to get to me," Caitlyn said. It had sounded a lot more reasonable when she considered the possibility last night. Now she just felt stupid—and ill for entirely different reasons.

"Wouldn't it make more sense to mimic someone you actually trust?" Nick sounded bitter. "Because that obviously isn't me."

Not knowing what else to say, Caitlyn sank into a nearby chair.

Nick sat across from her. "If anything, I should suspect you," he said. "Nobody died before you showed up."

Caitlyn's jaw tensed.

"Feels bad, doesn't it?" Nick leaned forward. "Caitlyn, tell me honestly," he continued in a gentler voice when Caitlyn raised her eyes to meet his. "Do you really think I'm a killer?"

"No, not really." Caitlyn sighed. "I just thought it would be irresponsible of me not to consider the possibility of a faerie pretending to be someone else to trick their victims. It's happened before."

"No, I think you were looking for excuses to avoid pursuing…whatever this thing we have going on is," Nick said.

"What thing?" Caitlyn stood back up. "We don't have a thing."

Nick rose to his feet. "I took you to dinner."

Caitlyn stared at him blankly.

"You know, a date? When you go out with someone you might like?" Nick sounded exasperated. "It typically leads to further dates unless something goes horribly wrong." He hesitated. "*Did* something go wrong? I'm a little rusty."

"You never said it was a date." Caitlyn felt a strong urge to tuck tail and run in the other direction, even more so than when she entertained the possibility Nick was the Vegas Ripper.

"Did I have to say it's a date for you to know it's a date?" Nick asked.

"In the age of 'it's complicated'?" Caitlyn retorted. "Yeah, kinda." She tried to smile but suspected it came out crooked. "I guess we're both a little rusty. I really am sorry that I—"

Something beeped.

Nick held up his index finger as he pulled his phone out of his pocket. "Dan's ready to cut his losses," he told Caitlyn after he typed something. "Tell you what. If you decide you want more practice, you know how to reach me."

Nick turned and left without another word.

"I'm such an idiot." Caitlyn said as she closed the door to her suite and leaned against it. Then she remembered she never did buy soda.

"Damn it!"

Caitlyn slid down the door until she sat on the hardwood floor. She decided to call it a night before she courted any more trouble.

chapter sixteen

"Any luck?"

Randy looked at Tiffany, his amber eyes tired and resigned. "Nope." He sat beside her on the sofa and leaned forward to pick up a breakfast sandwich off the table. "Any new intel from the wild kingdom?"

"I hate this," Tiffany said. "I don't want to just sit and wait for the next kill."

"I know," Randy said. "Anna really has ramped up security. I think your dancers are safe here. We can only hope our neighbors are taking the same precautions to protect their employees. And their guests, for that matter."

"Maybe we're safer because of the heightened Fae presence," Tiffany said. "Have you thought about scouting more than just Avalon at night?"

"It's worth considering," Randy said, "but unless I can pick up the killer's scent, I may as well be chasing wild geese—or however the saying goes." He paused, then perked up. "I never did visit the site of the most recent killing. Too much police activity. I doubt there's anything left that can lead me to the killer now, but I'll try to investigate tonight if things look quiet."

"And I guess I'll keep pretending everything's business as usual at rehearsal today. Might end up being a late night. We've started incorporating more of the moving set pieces so we may need to spend more time on blocking this week," Tiffany said. "I'll need to make sure everybody has safe transportation and nobody travels alone tonight especially."

Randy nodded. "Maybe it's better if I stay close to Avalon, then."

"Maybe," Tiffany conceded.

"The ratsss are up to sssomething," Perry said after Justin handed him to Tiffany.

"They're spying for my boss," Tiffany said under her breath. "There's a killer in town."

"Me?" Perry asked.

"No, not you!" Tiffany's eyes widened. Caitlyn and Amber both turned to look at her from their lyras. Even Justin and Miguel gave her strange looks. "Yes, you," Tiffany said as Miguel took away the python. "Sorry," she told Justin as he spun her into his arms. "Thought I was losing my grip. On Perry," she added.

Not reality, as she feared her dancers might be thinking.

"Snakes be slippery," Justin said, his tone mild.

Tiffany waited until everyone left the stage for a late lunch after the second act. Perry had been safely secured in his terrarium after they ran through "Free 2 Dance" a few times, but Tiffany thought she saw something small sneaking around backstage.

"Please don't be a fear sucker, please don't be a fear sucker," she whispered to herself when the lights reflected off a pair of beady black eyes. To her relief, a large brown rat hopped out of the shadows. "Hi," she said. "I don't know if you're the rat we talked to before, but if you have any news on the bad man, I'd love to hear it."

The rat stood up. "We think he's somewhere in the building, Miss. My brother was following him, but lost him in a crowd of people. I'm sorry. We try to avoid going anywhere people can see us."

Tiffany's heart sank into her stomach. "Does Morgan know?"

"She appeared to be eating dinner with a large group of men in business suits. They reeked of money and cheap cologne." The rat wrinkled his nose for emphasis.

"Who are you talking to?"

The rat ran away.

Tiffany turned to face Caitlyn. "I wasn't talking to anyone. I was just thinking out loud. It's been a long afternoon. I should get something to eat. Have you eaten?"

"I don't know what's weirder," Caitlyn said. "The fact you were talking to a rat, or the fact the rat appeared to be listening. I mean, I know they're supposed to be super smart, but—"

"My dad could communicate with other animals," Tiffany blurted out. "Now I can, too."

"Neat!" Caitlyn said. "Why didn't you tell me?"

"You don't think I'm crazy?" Tiffany asked.

"In the past few years, I've fought monsters and elementalists, and nearly had my life sucked out of me by some weird succubus-faerie type being. And, oh yeah—sidebar—a dragon once caught a nuke and launched it into another universe. No way could some fake that video without Industrial Light and Magic involved." Caitlyn said. "You being able to talk to rats is pretty mundane compared to dragons."

"When you put it that way," Tiffany chuckled, "it does sound a little mundane."

"I wouldn't go that far," Caitlyn said, "but we always expected new abilities to appear. Ooh, can you ask Gizmo if he misses me?"

Tiffany was about to answer when she remembered what the rat had told her before Caitlyn showed up. "I need to find Morgan," she said. "If I'm not back before lunch ends, can you tell everyone I needed to see Morgan about...I dunno, financial stuff?"

"What's wrong?" Caitlyn asked. "You look pale. Maybe you should eat first."

"No time," Tiffany told her. "I shouldn't say anything and you need to promise not to tell anyone so nobody panics, but the rats think the killer is in the building. They lost him in a crowd of people. Probably pretending to be a tourist or something."

"Or security," Caitlyn said.

"Or housekeeping." Tiffany's eyes widened as she considered all of the horrifying possibilities. Someone might invite him into their room being none-the-wiser.

"Go find Morgan," Caitlyn said. "I'll cover for you."

Tiffany found Anna in a private room in the steakhouse. With her hair hidden under a ballcap and sunglasses concealing her face, none of the patrons took any notice of the pop star. She peered at Anna through the window and hoped she'd be the first to notice Tiffany.

No such luck.

A heavyset man in an expensive suit glanced at her and said something to Anna.

He's here, Tiffany mouthed, hoping Anna understood the message. Then she remembered who she was dealing with. *The killer*, she thought, *he's somewhere in the building.* Anna must have heard her because she turned to Lance, who sat beside her, wearing a designer suit instead of his usual casual attire. He nodded and excused himself from the table.

"Let's talk," Lance said when he left the room. He led Tiffany through a door marked 'Employees only' and down the hall, away from the hustle and bustle of the restaurant staff. Nobody glanced in their direction, too busy with the early dinner rush.

"One of the rats saw him," Tiffany said. "He's getting bolder."

"I think he's toying with us," Lance said. "Wants us to know he's not afraid. Maybe it's a diversion, and he's targeting someone at a different hotel. But I'll alert security and Morgan's agents to his presence. Maybe we can catch him before he leaves."

"What should I do?" Tiffany asked.

"Whatever it takes to keep your crew and performers safe without alarming them," Lance said. "Leave everything else to security."

"Maybe I should end rehearsal early after all," Tiffany said.

"I don't think that's necessary," Lance said. "Not unless you were planning to work past midnight. He never strikes that early. Too many people. The important thing is everyone sticking together. Nobody walks alone."

chapter seventeen

Caitlyn was worried Tiffany would end rehearsal early, but when they took a late dinner break in the middle of blocking the third act, she knew she might have a chance to enact her plan after all. They didn't finish the third act until after ten.

"Stick with a buddy," Tiffany reminded the dancers as they started to leave the stage, but Caitlyn didn't budge.

"What are you doing?" Tiffany asked. "Aren't you tired?"

"I just want to run through 'Go Wild' another couple of times," Caitlyn said.

"But what about...*you know*," Tiffany said, casting furtive glances backstage.

"Crew's still cleaning up," Caitlyn told her. "I'll leave when they do. Promise."

"You better," Tiffany said, looking doubtful.

"Well, I'm certainly not sticking around after Joe turns off the lights," Caitlyn said. "Work lights will not be adequate. Besides, I still have PTSD from *Dracula*," she lied.

Finally, Tiffany left. All of the dancers and most of the crew were gone, too.

Joe agreed to lower Caitlyn's lyra.

"You only got about fifteen more minutes before it's lights out," he told her.

Ever since Tiffany told her Convict Two was in the building, Caitlyn knew what she had to do. Now she just needed to bide her time. She held onto the sides of the lyra and threw one leg over, then the other before pulling herself up.

"Five-minute warning!" Joe called from somewhere backstage after Caitlyn ran through her routine a couple times. He sounded like the real Joe, but Caitlyn considered the possibility he was the faerie in disguise. If so, she hoped the real Joe was safe, wherever he was. The imposter Joe would be in for a rough time if he gave Caitlyn the opportunity to use the toy surprise hidden under the sleeve of her off-shoulder sweatshirt.

"Cat, you're still here?"

Caitlyn paused, mid-pirouette. Amber stood offstage, a duffel bag slung over her shoulder. Like Caitlyn, she wore a sweatshirt over her leotard.

"I thought I was the last one left," Amber continued. "We should get going. It's late."

"Catch up with the others," Caitlyn said. "I can walk out with Joe."

"Suit yourself." Amber turned and walked away.

Caitlyn watched her leave, then hid between a couple flats backstage. She held her breath as Joe walked through with a flashlight. The pulley for her lyra was only a few feet away. Every second felt like an eternity as Joe raised the lyra. Finally, she heard footsteps and a side door open as he walked off stage. A few minutes later, the lights went out.

Caitlyn released a shaky breath. She walked onstage and sat on the floor. She took comfort in the feel of the leather sheath hiding the toy surprise against her skin. It wasn't really a toy, but a special faerie blade she saved from the time creepy Brendan had held Tiffany hostage in her own home. Caitlyn had used one to dispatch a reaver lurking in the backyard, but nobody knew she had a second hidden under her clothing.

A plan started taking shape as soon as Tiffany told Caitlyn the killer was in the hotel. Caitlyn had retrieved the blade from her nightstand during dinner and put on a sweatshirt to hide a sheath strapped to the inside of her wrist even though it made for an awkward uncomfortable rehearsal. Caitlyn didn't know if the killer would take the bait, but she decided to try.

As Caitlyn sat in the dark, the sides of the stage lit only by dim work lights, she wondered how long she should wait. *Maybe I should go into the dressing room instead,* she thought. *Or the stairwell?*

An alarm sounded before Caitlyn could decide her next move, and all the emergency lights turned on in the theater.

Fire?

No, this alarm sounded like a wail, not a high-pitched beeping sound.

Caitlyn ran backstage, out a side door, and down the hall to her dressing room. Her bag was slowly bouncing off the counter due to the vibrations of something contained within. Sure enough, Caitlyn had an alert on her phone from Avalon Security advising her to shelter in place. She heard footsteps racing down the hall. Someone pounded on the dressing room door.

"Is anyone in there?"

Caitlyn recognized the voice, but couldn't place it.

"Only me," she shouted back.

Caitlyn knew there was a chance the speaker was the killer and not security, but luring the killer into a trap had been her plan all along, so she readied herself to draw her weapon as the doorknob turned.

chapter eighteen

"Cat, what the hell are you still doing here?"

An imposing Black woman in a black suit stood in the doorway. She raised an eyebrow.

Agent Cook!

Caitlyn hadn't seen the faerie agent since Los Angeles.

"I was getting ready to leave when the alarm sounded," Caitlyn lied. "What's going on?"

"Convict Two attacked a dancer in the stairwell," Agent Cook told her.

Oh no. Caitlyn's heart sank into her stomach. *Amber. You let her go alone.*

"Agent Baker almost had him, but he got away," Agent Cook said.

"And the dancer?"

"Still alive," Agent Cook said. "Agent Baker had to choose between helping her and going after Convict Two. He might have injured his leg. Agent Baker heard something crack when he kicked him during the struggle."

Still alive, Caitlyn thought wonderingly. *Please be okay, Amber.*

"All stairwells confirmed clear," came a voice over the walkie talkie Agent Cook held in her right hand. "That leaves the Otherworld Theater and the backstage areas."

"Otherworld Theater and the backstage areas are clear," Agent Cook said into the walkie talkie, "apart from one snake and one dancer, identity confirmed."

"Agent Green successfully slowed the bleeding and performed a healing incantation before the ambulance arrived," Caitlyn heard Agent Baker say. "The victim is now en route to the hospital, but she's already lost a lot of blood."

"Thank you, Agent Baker," said another voice over the walkie talkie. *Morgan perhaps?* "Agent Cook, debrief the dancer and escort them back to their room. I'll let security know they can push a new message ending the shelter in place. I want all agents to report back to me."

"It's probably a good thing it's just me hearing all of that," Caitlyn said, "and not a less informed dancer."

Agent Cook gave her a withering stare. "Look. I don't know what you were doing here alone, but we aren't in Hollywood anymore. I never would've let you help then had I known what we were up against. Now give me back that knife you're hiding up your sleeve and let's go."

Caitlyn sighed. She rolled up her sleeve to remove the sheath strapped to her arm and laid it across Agent Cook's palm.

Emi and Jade were sitting on chairs in the common area when Caitlyn arrived on her floor. Emi jumped up and through her arms around her. "Cat, we were so worried!"

"Where's Amber?" Jade asked, her forehead wrinkled.

Agent Cook spared Caitlyn from having to answer. "A dancer was injured in the stairwell tonight. She's on her way to the hospital now. Does Amber have blond hair? Was she wearing a gray sweatshirt over a pink one-piece leotard?"

Jade nodded, eyes wide and bright.

Emi burst into tears. Caitlyn patted her back. She looked at Agent Cook's stern face over Emi's shoulder and wished for a hole to open in the floor and swallow herself whole…but then, that would endanger Emi, too. Some friend Caitlyn was; always thinking of herself first before considering the consequences for others.

"I think she's going to make it," Agent Cook said in a gruff voice, sounding uncomfortable. "You should all get some rest. We'll know more in the morning."

Emi let go of Caitlyn and took a deep shaky breath before turning away to walk back to her room. Jade glanced at Caitlyn, a single tear tracing a line through a hint of blush, then walked back to her own room.

"Thanks," Caitlyn told Agent Cook in a tentative voice.

He gave her a long look behind his dark sunglasses but left without another word.

Loud knocking woke Caitlyn from a light sleep. She pulled on a pair of shorts under her oversized tee and left the bedroom to peer out the peephole.

Uh oh.

"Agent Baker, what a pleasant surprise!"

WHAT THE HELL DID YOU THINK YOU WERE DOING?

Agent Baker's voice thundered in her head, as a courtesy to other people staying on the same floor, perhaps? She felt too shaken by this new development to know how to respond. *Should I think my answer or say it aloud…?*

"Well?"

"I heard a rumor the killer was in the hotel and I thought if I was alone, he would come after me and I would know how to deal with him," Caitlyn said.

"And instead, he went after someone else. I felt her life running out of her body, Caitlyn. He sliced her carotid artery clean through. Had someone other than the Fae found her, she'd be dead right now. That could have been you."

"She's my friend." Caitlyn felt her eyes fill with tears. "She's my friend, and I let her leave the theater alone because I took for granted that she'd be safe. I was so sure he would come for me because…"

Because why?

Because someone called me a fae magnet once, and I took it to heart?

You are not *the main character,* Caitlyn reminded herself.

"And what made you think you'd fare any better?" Agent Baker asked.

"I kept a knife," Caitlyn muttered. "When we saved Tiffany. I killed a reaver then, and I've even fought off soul eaters when all I had was a prop sword."

"A knife? Where?" Agent Baker stormed past Caitlyn to open drawers in the kitchen.

"Agent Cook already took it back," Caitlyn said. She walked to the sofa and sat down, hugging her legs against her chest and resting her head on her knees.

Agent Baker stopped searching and walked in front of the sofa. "I'm sorry about your friend, but hopefully you now understand why you need to stop playing detective and let us handle him ourselves. Of all the convicts, he may be the most dangerous. So dangerous we were supposed to work in pairs, but we were an agent short. I broke his leg, and still he got away."

Caitlyn lifted her head off her knees. "How do you know he broke his leg? Maybe you just bruised the bone." She couldn't imagine someone escaping with a broken leg, even a faerie.

"I *saw* the bone," Agent Baker said.

Caitlyn's stomach turned. "Can he heal himself?"

"We can heal faster than humans," Agent Baker said, "but he's not a healer himself, no. We suspect he will be laying low for a while. I wouldn't be surprised if he leaves town and resumes killing women someplace else."

"Why does he do it?"

"Because he can," Agent Baker said. "He's cruel and sadistic, and the last time he did it, he chose victims he thought nobody would miss. Your world has changed some since then, but not enough, and not everywhere. There are places he can go that will attract less media attention. I don't think he was ready for that, but now that he knows, he'll avoid big cities."

"And you'll be back to square one," Caitlyn said.

"I don't think he'll move on until he's healed," Agent Baker said. "We still have time, but we can't have any more interference from humans in over their heads."

"Understood."

Caitlyn did not sleep well after Agent Baker left. She felt horrible about Amber, but something else kept gnawing at her brain. If Convict Two didn't want to be caught, why did he try to kill someone in Avalon of all places?

Arrogance?

Or something else?

Caitlyn forced herself to push thoughts of Convict Two out of her mind. Agent Baker was right. Not only was she to blame for leaving Amber alone, she realized she may have been the reason Convict Two got away.

Time to back off before anyone else got hurt.

chapter nineteen

Tiffany couldn't sleep. She tried to find out Amber's status at the hospital, but of course they wouldn't talk to friends, not even a celebrity like Tiffany Sharp, only family. She had contacted Mr. and Mrs. Mills at their home in Maitland, Florida. They were distraught but grateful after Tiffany used her travel agent to secure a ride for them to the airport in Orlando and a redeye to Las Vegas, all at her own expense. Somehow their gratitude made her feel worse.

"You've done all you can for now," Randy told her.

Tiffany stood in the window looking down at the strip, as if she could see Convict Two limping somewhere in the shadows if she stared hard enough. Randy wrapped his arms around her waist, resting his head on one of her shoulders.

"I didn't do enough, and now Amber's hurt. She could have died. She still might!"

"We'll know more in the morning," Randy said. "You need to be up early to meet her family at the airport, remember?" He kissed the crook of Tiffany's neck, then let go of her waist to climb back into bed.

"I know," Tiffany sighed. She crawled into bed beside Randy and turned on her side. He slid an arm under her pillow and pulled her close with the other. Soon she dozed off, but her dreams were filled with blood and monsters.

. . .

A bleary-eyed Tiffany stood at the arrivals gate at the airport the next morning. Randy stayed outside in a nondescript rental SUV with an extra row of seats. She hid her brown waves under a baseball cap and wore oversized sunglasses and a baggy sweatshirt over jeans.

When the Mills' flight arrived, they were the first to deplane. Though she had never met them before, Tiffany recognized Amber's parents right away. Her mother had the same beautiful blond hair, only shoulder-length, and her father was clearly the source of Amber's strong jaw and warm brown eyes. A teenage girl walked beside them, tightlipped with brown chin-length hair and blue eyes like Mrs. Mills.

"You're shorter than I thought you'd be," she said when Tiffany stepped forward to greet Amber's parents.

"Sienna," chided Mrs. Mills.

"It's fine," Tiffany said. "It's probably the shoes. I perform in heels, but I wear flats the rest of the time. Helps me blend in with the crowd."

"Right," Sienna said. "The sunglasses inside are really inconspicuous."

"We all handle our anxiety in different ways," Mr. Mills said by way of apology.

"Morgan offered a suite in Avalon," Tiffany said, "but I thought you'd prefer staying closer to the hospital. I've already made arrangements if that's okay."

"Oh, you've done so much for us already," Mrs. Mills said. "I don't want to impose any more on your kindness."

"It's the least I can do," Tiffany said. "Truly."

Tiffany offered to drop the Mills family off at the hospital, but they asked if she wanted to come in, so now she sat in the waiting room with Sienna and Randy while Amber's parents talked to the doctors.

"How'd the killer get in, anyway?" Sienna asked in a low voice. "Isn't Morgan le Fay supposed to be, like, the most powerful being on the planet?"

"I dunno," Tiffany said, looking to Randy for help. He looked as disarmed as she felt. "Avalon has really good security, but I guess it wasn't enough."

"Saved her life, anyway," Sienna said. "The other women weren't so lucky." She looked up at Tiffany, her eyes shining with unshed tears. "Will Amber be able to perform again?"

Tiffany's eyes widened. She was so worried about whether or not Amber would survive, she hadn't even considered the possibility of a career-ending injury. To her surprise, Sienna's hand found her own.

"I don't like your music," Sienna said, "but I can tell you care about my sister. Thank you."

Mr. and Mrs. Mills returned to the waiting room after an hour or so had passed. "Sienna, your mom can take you to visit your sister," Mr. Mills said, "but she's very weak and tired. She may not stay awake for long and she...she can't really talk."

Sienna stood and gave Tiffany a little wave.

"The hospital thinks it will be a few days before she can handle any other visitors," Mr. Mills said to Tiffany after Sienna walked away with a tearful Mrs. Mills, "but I know she appreciates you being here. We all do. I need to talk to someone about insurance now."

"Avalon and myself are prepared to take full financial responsibility," Tiffany said. "Morgan and I consider it a work-related injury, so our lawyers and accountants will be in communication with the hospital every step of the way. We don't want your family to worry about anything but Amber's healing."

Mr. Mills took one of Tiffany's hands in both of his own. "I have to admit, our family was never fully comfortable with Amber continuing to work for you after...well, everything people know now, but she always defended you." He paused, visibly choked up. "I can see how you earned her loyalty."

Tiffany bowed her head.

Would the Mills feel the same way if they knew about the killer's origin?

"Thank you," she said. "I need to get back to Avalon, but Randy is on his way back with a set of keys and the paperwork for your rental car. It's yours for as long as you need it."

"Speak of the devil," Mr. Mills said, smiling through his tears. He patted Randy on the shoulder. Randy handed him the rental car keys and paperwork.

"Is it alright with the family that I update my crew and performers on Amber's status?" Tiffany asked.

"Of course," Mr. Mills said. "According to her doctors, her condition is stable. The blood transfusion was successful. They're just monitoring for any adverse reactions. They expect some scarring to her neck, but the biggest remaining concern is her voice. You see, the attacker—he severed her vocal cords…"

Tiffany maintained her composure up until the moment she climbed back into the SUV beside Randy. He didn't say anything, just let her cry as he drove back to Avalon. After they returned to their suite, she dried her eyes and prepared to meet with the crew and performers. She didn't bother putting on any makeup. She doubted it would do anything to help her red eyes and blotchy face anyway.

The crew and performers didn't look much better when Tiffany addressed them from the Otherworld Theater stage. Randy remained at her side for support. In a rare public appearance, "Morgan" stood to her other side, dressed simply in a black satin shirt and dark jeans, her auburn hair falling down her back in loose curls. More than a few members of the audience stared at Tiffany's benefactor with eyes full of awe and reverence.

"The good news is, Amber is going to make it," Tiffany told the audience. Everyone clapped, and a few even cheered. She saw Emi and Jade hug each other in the first row. Caitlyn sat beside them, staring at her hands in her lap.

"What's the bad news?" someone shouted several rows back.

"Doctors don't know if Amber will recover the full use of her voice," Tiffany said. Audible gasps filled the room. "We're pausing rehearsals for at least a week. When we know more, we may be holding auditions to replace Amber. You will still be paid in the interim. If anyone wants to bow out, I understand. Avalon will release you from your contracts and provide an additional month's pay, no harm, no foul."

Murmurs in the audience grew louder. "Morgan and I will stick around as long as necessary to talk to anyone about your concerns," Tiffany said in a louder voice. "Otherwise, the rest of the day is now your own."

To Tiffany's surprise, none of the crew and few performers chose to leave the production. Not yet, anyway. She saw Caitlyn hanging back. The anxious woman looked like she wanted to tell Tiffany something, but slipped out before the last of the crew and performers left.

chapter twenty

S o many people had gasped when Tiffany said Amber may not regain the use of her voice. Emi openly sobbed while Jade consoled her, but Caitlyn could only sit, frozen in place. *All my fault,* her brain repeated on a loop. *It's all my fault.*

If Amber wouldn't be able to perform, neither should Caitlyn, but she couldn't bring herself to confront Tiffany and drop out of the show.

Instead, she slunk away like the coward she was and went back to her room to doze on the sofa while a marathon of that stupid *Love in Paradise* played on the television. Her only other choices were talk shows and "news" networks that would surely be talking about the Vegas Ripper, especially now that they had the Tiffany Sharp connection to lean into.

Caitlyn didn't know how many hours had passed when someone knocked on the door. She forced herself off the sofa to see who it was. Not Emi or Jade, she hoped. Or Tiffany.

It wasn't any of the three.

Caitlyn opened the door. "Nick, what are you—"

He pulled Caitlyn into a tight hug before she could finish the question.

"When I heard the Vegas Ripper attacked a dancer at Avalon, I was so scared it was you," Nick said, his voice muffled by her messy hair. "Honestly, I'm a little surprised the front desk gave me your room number. You should talk to security about that. It's not safe."

Nick loosened his hold to stare into Caitlyn's bleary eyes.

She took one look at his earnest face and did the one thing she almost never did, especially in front of other people—not even when she broke up with boyfriends or when Tiffany kicked her out because that creep Brendan had framed her for leaking rumors to the media.

Caitlyn started to cry.

Nick pulled her in close again and awkwardly patted her back.

"He hurt my friend," Caitlyn sputtered between sobs, "and it's all my fault. You're supposed to stick together. No matter what. I learned that the hard way in New York, but still I screwed up."

She let Nick guide her to the sofa, and they sat down. "How did you screw up?" he asked.

"I let Amber leave the theater alone because I knew the killer was in the building and I thought I could lure him into a trap," Caitlyn said. "I've done some dumb things in my life, but this is the first time I've ever endangered someone else."

"You tried to use yourself as bait?" Nick sounded incredulous. "Are you insane?"

"Clearly," she said, bursting into a fresh round of tears.

Nick handed her a tissue from the table. Caitlyn took it and walked into the kitchen to blow her nose. She took a fresh dishcloth and wet it down to wipe her face before returning to the sofa.

"Caitlyn, listen to me." Nick placed a hand against Caitlyn's cheek and gently turned her head to face him. "You made a bad call, but you can't blame yourself for what happened to your friend. I mean, you can," he continued when she tried to protest, "but it's not going to fix the past. You just have to do better next time."

Caitlyn nodded, sniffling.

"You know, for being all pale and blotchy, you're still the prettiest girl in town."

Before Caitlyn could remind Nick about Tiffany Sharp and every other gorgeous woman she saw every day, he leaned in to kiss her. She closed her eyes. Muscle memory could be funny like that. Caitlyn felt a jolt down her spine when his lips brushed against hers. She pulled away, surprised by her body's response to the kiss.

"I'm sorry," Nick said. "I was out of line."

"No, no," Caitlyn said. "It's been sort of a crazy day. It happens."

"Is that all it was?" Nick sounded sad. "I should get going. Almost time to start my shift." He stood up. "I'm glad you're safe, Caitlyn. The world's a brighter place with you in it." When she didn't answer, he let himself out.

Caitlyn stared at the door, wondering what the hell just happened.

It wasn't even their first kiss, but Caitlyn had been swept up in a different set of emotions then, between a breakup and the apparent end of her Broadway career before it even began—to say nothing of a particularly buzzy buzz from drowning her sorrows in one too many cocktails.

It didn't mean anything then, and it doesn't mean anything now, Caitlyn tried to convince herself, but the residual tingling sensation said otherwise. She picked up a throw pillow and screamed into it before falling back against the couch. For a moment, she'd forgotten all about Amber, but now a new wave of guilt pushed aside her confusion over Nick.

Caitlyn continued to doze on the sofa. Emi and Jade stopped by at some point, but she ignored them and went back to sleep. Some dreams were better than others. She didn't know how many hours had passed the next time someone knocked on the door, interrupting a dream that made her blush as she recalled the hazy details.

For a moment, Caitlyn sat in the darkness, feeling more than a little confused and disoriented until someone knocked again. She wondered if Nick had returned after his shift and her blush deepened, but she heard a rumble of thunder in the distance as she stumbled into the dining room and turned on the light over the table. Not late, just stormy. The microwave clock in the kitchenette confirmed the time: seven-thirty in the evening.

Caitlyn held on to a sliver of hope as she looked out the peephole. She tried to hide her disappointment when she opened the door.

"You're not going to quit on me, are you, Cat?" Tiffany walked into Caitlyn's suite with a box of pizza. "Emi and Jade had a feeling you were holed up in here when you didn't answer the door earlier. So I thought you might be hungry." She set the box down on the dining table.

"I'm not going to quit," Caitlyn told her, "but you might fire me after I tell you what happened last night."

"You mean trying to use yourself as bait?" Tiffany said. "Agents Baker and Cook think you learned your lesson, so I'm not going to hold it against you. Just promise me you won't do anything stupid like that again. Losing Amber is bad enough."

"But it's my fault you lost Amber," Caitlyn said. "I let her go alone."

"She wasn't alone," Tiffany said. "I saw the security footage. She left with other people, but the elevators were full. It looked like she decided to use the stairwell instead of waiting for the next one. Maybe things would've gone differently had you been there, but the only person to blame is Convict Two."

Caitlyn frowned, unconvinced.

"Look," Tiffany said, "it's probably going to be a few days before friends can visit Amber in the hospital, but you need to let her decide if blame is in order. Beating yourself up over what happened doesn't help anyone. At least that's what Randy keeps saying." She walked into the kitchenette for paper plates and peeked between the blinds of a window above the sink that overlooked the strip.

Caitlyn sat down at the dining table. "What's it like out there, anyway? Media circus?"

A flash of lightning lit up the suite before Tiffany answered. "Until the clouds started rolling in. Morgan is handling most of it." She sat across from Caitlyn at the dining table. "They asked me about the future of the show, and I told them our first priority is Amber's recovery. Then they asked Morgan how the killer got past security. She pointed out that her team is the reason Amber is still alive." Tiffany paused when thunder rumbled outside. "Oh, and she used her, uh, powers of persuasion to talk the police down from questioning a bunch of people. Thanks to security footage, they know they're looking for a man with a limp, for all the good it does if he goes into hiding. I think the forensics team is still around collecting evidence."

Caitlyn took out a single slice of pizza. "Are you really going to replace Amber?"

"I don't want to," Tiffany said, "but we have to hold auditions in a week or two regardless because some performers took me up on my offer." She took a slice for herself. "I don't blame them, but I doubt Convict Two would be so brazen as to attack someone here again."

"If I were Convict Two, I'd find the nearest vortex off the planet," Caitlyn said. She took a bite of pizza as she contemplated his motivation.

"Then again, I wouldn't be a homicidal killer in the first place," she said after she finished chewing.

Tiffany nodded. "Imagine having all that power and using it to kill defenseless women in dark alleys." She pushed her plate away, looking pensive. "Brendan let his power drive him mad, too, and he was only part-Fae, like me."

"Well, your dad was all Fae, and he was a good guy. So is Morgan," Caitlyn said. "Just warn me if animals start telling you to kill people."

Another flash of lightning. Thunder soon followed.

"Deal," Tiffany said.

chapter twenty-one

B rian Evans sat at an outdoor bar on Fremont Street nursing a Gold Rush. He just picked the first bourbon-based cocktail on the list. It also had honey, lemon, and, in keeping with the perpetual party vibe of the old strip, edible glitter. He'd missed the mention of glitter on the drink menu. Oh well. Not like he was worried about anyone claiming his man card.

Brian wasn't particularly large, but he was wiry and well-muscled. The newish scar that started above his eyebrow and ended above one of his cheekbones lent him an air of mystery and danger. Little did people around here know that he'd earned the scar from a chance encounter with an unknown primate-like animal on another world, and not a knife fight like many assumed. His girl Simone assured him he was still pretty but asked him to stop playing with the local fauna until she pinpointed the best flora to treat any mystery infections. The wound healed cleanly enough thanks to butterfly bandages and a healing ointment from home, but Brian wasn't in a hurry to climb any trees surrounding their settlement again anytime soon.

Brian wasn't in a hurry to see Black Anna either, but he knew he couldn't put it off any longer. An unknown man in a familiar black suit had reached out to Brian because the faerie queen needed to see him about an urgent matter. Little did she know Brian had his own news to share from the Council. He'd planned to go to Avalon yesterday, but it was crawling with cops and reporters after a dancer was attacked by an apparent serial killer. Brian had a sneaking suspicion the killer was one of the Fae. Who else could sneak past Avalon's defenses?

Doctors expected the latest victim to survive, but other dancers had been less lucky, and the police weren't making any headway. No shocker there, but Brian would have expected Anna to fare better than local authorities. Then again, with Morgan missing and Anna assuming control of both the Lafayette Corporation and the Lafayette Foundation, Anna might be in over her head.

Bureaucracy?

Not her strong suit.

That's why Anna left most decisions up to the Council.

And then there were the rumblings about New York State possibly releasing Emerson Fowler on a technicality despite charges of multiple counts of conspiracy and kidnapping. Allegations of human trafficking didn't stick because would-be victims like Simone hadn't been available to testify. The cult had sacrificed Simone and other foster children to a mysterious entity in exchange for wealth and power. Little did Emerson know, the entity had been Anna. Instead of killing children, she took them to a new world uninhabited by other sentient beings.

Unless you counted vicious tree-dwelling furballs like the creature that cut Brian's face open. He realized he was rubbing at his scar.

Brian considered reaching out to his sister Bianca. The last time they talked was last Christmas. He tried to convince her to join them in the other world, but she was building a life for herself in Rochester, a little too close to Emerson Fowler's old stomping grounds for Brian's comfort level. Bianca had run afoul of the construction mogul searching for Brian.

After he was separated from his sister following their mother's death, Brian lived in the same foster home as Simone. When Simone disappeared, Brian ran away to find her. His investigation led him to Anna. Bianca's investigation led her to a Lafayette home in Western New York after Emerson's cult attempted to frame them. Their paths converged when Emerson abducted a child from a park in Buffalo in an act of desperation.

Anna saw that the girl was returned to her family, police found enough evidence to charge Emerson and other cult members, and Emerson maintained that the Lafayette Foundation was framing *him*. It was always projection with those people. Brian knew Emerson harbored a grudge against his sister, too, even though Bianca never completed a planned documentary about her investigation. Maybe the threat of retribution from Emerson would be enough to make Bianca reconsider her objections to leaving this broken world behind.

"Any fun plans today?" a green-eyed bartender asked Brian when he closed his tab after one drink and an order of chicken wings.

"Not so much," Brian said. He left a generous tip and headed for the designated ride-sharing spot. Brian pulled his hood over his short black hair as it started to rain. At least he had an excuse to wear a hoodie. Now that Bianca knew the truth, nobody was looking for Brian anymore, but he still preferred to keep a low profile when he visited the home planet—as Simone mockingly called it. She came back for the rare trip to restock medical supplies, but mostly, she sent others with a list of what she needed. The more the settlers learned about their new world, the less she needed from here.

Brian's ride pulled up to the curb just as it started to hail. His driver, Hector, wasn't a talker. Brian didn't mind. It was a short trip to Avalon, anyway. He took off his sunglasses but kept his hood up when he entered the hotel.

Nobody paid Brian any attention as he walked to the elevators, but a little kid stared while they waited. "What happened to your eye?"

"Cole, we don't ask strangers questions like that," the kid's mother said.

"It's okay," Brian said. "Got in a fight with a squirrel monkey over some fruit."

Now the mother stared. She appeared uncertain as her gaze turned to the empty elevator reaching their floor

"It's a'ight," Brian said. "I'll get the next one."

The mother dragged Cole into the elevator without another glance at Brian.

Brian had the next elevator to himself. He pulled a wrinkled business card out of his back pocket and flipped it over to read the first code hastily scrawled on the back. Brian typed the code into the keypad to reach the lowest level of Avalon. He needed another code when he reached the bottom-most floor.

As soon as Brian stepped into a long hallway lit only by soft lavender track lighting, some unseen force barreled into him, knocking him to the floor.

"Hold up," said a familiar voice. "That's not an intruder. Brian, how are you?"

Lance leaned forward to offer Brian a hand and pull him to his feet.

"Black man in a hoodie and you automatically assume I'm an intruder?" Brian turned around to look for his assailant. He patted himself down, checking for broken ribs. Whoever it was hit like a Mack truck.

"We couldn't see your face in the security camera, and a young woman was attacked in the stairwell two nights ago," said the stern woman who materialized in front of Brian. "You'll have to excuse us if we're a little on edge."

"Yes, ma'am," Brian said. He'd forgotten how much the Fae varied in physical appearance, even though he knew they all had the same eerie translucent skin behind their illusions to capture as much dying sunlight in their own world as possible.

"Thank you, Susan," Lance told the woman. "I've got it from here." He led Brian into a large office.

A large leather chair faced away from the oak desk in the center of the room. Its occupant swiveled around to face Brian. "Morgan" squealed and jumped out of the chair. She ran around the desk to give Brian a hug as her hair changed from auburn to black. She wore a black sleeveless dress that stopped above her knees and heels. Clearly Anna was taking liberties with her sister's more business-like style.

"I've missed you so much!" Anna looked up at Brian with her doe eyes. "How's Simone? Has she finally worn down all your silly little defenses?"

Brian couldn't help but chuckle. "I never stood a chance, did I?"

Anna squealed again and clapped her hands. Then she turned serious. "Oh, Brian, everything's such a mess. I can't wait until we figure out where Morgan went and I can be done with all this..." She gestured at a messy pile of papers on her desk. "Whatever it is," she finished. "I don't know what I'd do without Lance to help me make sense of everything. Maybe you can fill in for a few days," she told Lance, "So I can go back with Brian to visit."

"About that..." Brian hesitated. Anna had never been anything but kind to Brian, but she could be mercurial and unpredictable under the best of circumstances.

"I think Susan might need me," Lance said. "To help monitor the live video feeds." He pulled the doors shut from the outside.

Brian turned back to Anna. "The Council recently had a vote, and, well...as long as Morgan is missing, they think it's best you don't come back. If someone did something to her and they come for you next, they're worried it might jeopardize everything you've built."

"Right." Anna sat down behind her desk. "You say 'they,' but you're on the Council, too."

Brian knew that was coming. "I abstained from the vote," he said. "To avoid a tie."

"I suppose I don't need to know any more than that," Anna said. "After all, everyone just wants to protect what I...what *we* have built." She paused, her brow furrowing. "Aren't they worried you might lead an unwelcome visitor back yourself?"

"It was a calculated risk," Brian said. "Now why did you summon me?"

"I'm worried it might be a moot point now," Anna said. "One of Tiffany Sharp's backup singers saw a boy on Fremont Street the other day. An elementalist. He's only a teenager, and he has a little sister. He performs tricks for tips to keep her fed. They appear to be living on the street. I was wondering if maybe you'd be able to take them with you. An agent keeping tabs on them hasn't seen any sign of other adults."

"Which element?"

"Fire..."

"Fire," Brian repeated. "Of course it's fire. Like the pyromancer who almost turned my sister and I into great big piles of ash when they came to Chateau Beaumont looking for that dragon. I know we accept all kinds, Anna, but we live in the middle of a great big forest, and all our homes are made out of wood, and pyromancers aren't exactly known for being chill."

"Chill!" Anna giggled. "I see what you did there."

Brian remained stone-faced.

"Oh, Brian, they're just children," Anna said.

"Why not let them stay here?" Brian asked. "Maybe he can heat up Tiffany's show."

Anna made a face. "I mean…well, Avalon's made out of wood, too, mostly. I think. I guess I have my own reservations. Is it still raining?"

"Off and on," Brian said. "Probably not the most favorable conditions for pyromancy."

Anna sighed. "Guess I know what I'm doing today." Her lip curled as she regarded her messy desk. "My paperwork can wait." Her expression softened, the hint of a smile betraying her lack of disappointment over the change in plans.

Brian grinned. Bianca's filmmaker friend had once referred to Anna as Scary Poppins, but she liked kids as much as she hated paperwork.

"How long do you think you'll be around?" Anna asked. She didn't clarify if she meant Las Vegas, or the planet.

"Dunno," Brian said. "Keeping tabs on the Emerson Fowler situation."

"Lance doesn't like leaving the east coast shorthanded, but the situation here is so volatile," Anna said. "I really, really wish I knew where Morgan was. Take care of yourself, Brian. Maybe next time we'll be meeting under more favorable circumstances."

"See you around, Anna." Brian held out his fist.

Anna bumped it, then threw her arms around him for another hug.

chapter twenty-two

Tiffany looked down at Randy's prone form in the bed as he slept. Apart from sharing dinner before he left and breakfast when he returned, she felt like they never had any time to themselves. Convict Two dominated most of their conversions. Tiffany knew Randy wouldn't rest until they found Convict Two, even though his trail had gone cold. Morgan's agents predicted Convict Two wouldn't be ready to move on for at least a couple weeks while his leg healed unless he decided to take his chances in some other world.

The hotel's rat colony, not just a mischief but a whole colony of rats, scoured the streets of Las Vegas in search of Convict Two. If they couldn't find Morgan, they updated Tiffany on their progress, or lack thereof. Gizmo's wild eyes just about popped out of his head this morning when one appeared from beneath the sofa, but the Devon rex had enough sense to leave it alone as it conversed with Tiffany.

"I remember when you used to have standards for the company you kept," Groucho Manx had said with disdain in between grooming himself on her nightstand with one leg stretched high into the air.

"I remember when you kept your snide remarks to yourself," she told him.

Groucho Manx had merely turned his back on Tiffany and curled into a ball.

Someone knocked on the door.

Groucho Manx opened one eye. Tiffany felt him watching as she walked out of the bedroom. She heard a thump as he dropped to the floor to follow.

"*Morgan*! To what do I owe the pleasure?" Tiffany stepped aside as Anna strode into the room. Today she appeared almost casual in a red blouse that fell from one shoulder, dark-washed jeans, and black high heels.

"Is that what you're wearing?" Anna looked at Tiffany's oversized sweatshirt—Randy's, actually—and apparent bare legs. She did have on running shorts, but the sweatshirt skimmed the bottom.

"I haven't really dressed for the day," Tiffany said. "I've been waiting for Amber's parents to call with any updates. Not that I expected to hear anything yet, but with rehearsals temporarily paused, I haven't really decided how to use my free time. I should probably be writing."

"Writing can wait," Anna said. "We're going on a mission."

Tiffany raised an eyebrow.

"So, it turns out the Council has concerns about bringing in any newcomers, especially with Morgan missing and a homicidal faerie on the loose," Anna said. "Looks like it's up to me to provide a safe haven to those elementalist children. Since your schedule is wide open, and everyone else is busy looking for Convict Two or managing day-to-day operations, I thought you could join me on Fremont Street. After all, you've been there. I rarely leave Avalon."

"Aren't you worried about drawing a crowd?"

"Oh, I've got that covered." Anna pulled a pair of oversized sunglasses out of her satchel. Her hair changed from auburn to a lighter strawberry blond.

"Just give me a minute to get ready," Tiffany told her, hiding a smile. She went into the bedroom and changed into jeans and a loose black tee shirt, then pulled her brown hair into a ponytail and tucked it under a baseball cap. She retrieved her own pair of oversized sunglasses from the counter in the bathroom before rejoining Anna.

. . .

Outside, the sun occasionally peeked through the clouds. A light rain fell. Though the stormy weather provided a temporary reprieve from the hot summer air as July transitioned into August, the humidity made Tiffany's hair curl and frizz. Anna arranged for an understated sedan to drop them off near Fremont Street.

It was less congested than Tiffany's last visit, but not by much. Despite the periodic rain, she spotted a small crowd around a teenage boy with dark hair and tawny skin.

"There he is," Anna said.

The elementalist juggled three fiery orbs while people gasped and cheered.

"What should we do?" she asked, turning to Tiffany.

"Wait and see if he takes a break?"

Tiffany checked the time. It was early afternoon. If he'd already had lunch, they might be waiting awhile. She led Anna to an outdoor café. They sat at a table for two under a red umbrella that gave them a clear view of the elementalist. A server came to take their orders. Tiffany ordered lemonades and turkey sandwiches for both of them.

Anna never took her eyes off the elementalist. "You know," she said after the server returned with their lemonades, "I think Brian might've been on to something. That boy would make a fine addition for your show. Or maybe he can be the opening act."

Tiffany felt too taken aback to ask who Brian was. Anna's contact from her settlement, she assumed. Instead, she said, "I did have one of my fire eaters bow out the other day, but this boy is just a kid. Besides, he's not exactly from around here. I think he might be overwhelmed."

"He seems to be adapting to this world just fine," Anna said. The crowd oohed and aahed as the elementalist appeared to manipulate a larger orb of fire like a rhythmic gymnast only centimeters from his exposed shoulders. "I'm sure a guaranteed paycheck and housing would take the edge off performing for a larger audience."

Tiffany found it hard to argue with that. The problem remained how long they would have to wait and how they should approach the elementalist. They barely had time to finish their food and pay before the elementalist took a bow and disappeared into the crowd.

"I think I see him," Anna said. "In line at that hot dog vendor."

Anna ran off to chase him, and Tiffany hurried after her.

The elementalist had just reached into his pocket to pay for two hot dogs when Anna cut in front of him. "I'm paying," she said, handing a wad of cash to the hot dog vendor. "Keep the change."

The elementalist's dark eyes widened. He ducked back into the crowd with his hot dogs.

"Hey, you overpaid me by ten bucks," the vendor called out, but Anna was already chasing after the boy. Her high heels barely slowed her down as she kept pace with him as easily as Tiffany could in sneakers. They followed him into a narrow alleyway.

"Are you cops?" he asked, turning to face them. "You don't look like cops."

"We're not cops," Tiffany told him.

"We want to offer you a job, and a place to stay," Anna said.

"You ran after me to offer me a job?" The boy asked, raising an eyebrow. He no longer looked frightened, only confused.

"We ran after you because you ran away before we could offer you a job, silly," Anna said.

"How long have you been here?" Tiffany asked. "You speak our language so well."

"How did you...?" The boy paused, his distrust returning.

"We know what you are," Anna said. "I'm not exactly from around here, myself," she added, her hair changing from strawberry blond to auburn. "And we know you're here alone, except for a little girl you take care of. She's probably hungry. Her food is getting cold."

Tiffany was worried about pushing him too far, but something about Anna's gentle smile seemed to put the boy at ease despite her illusions.

"Follow me," he said as he led them around the corner to another alley. "Zaya, you can come out. They won't hurt us."

A little girl appeared from behind a dumpster. She looked the same as Caitlyn had described her. Dark hair and eyes like her brother, only her hair fell in a tangle of curls, tawny skin, and an oversized tee shirt that reached the tops of her knees. Mismatched shoes, too. One dirty white sneaker, one black ballet flat losing the leather on the toe.

The boy handed her a hot dog. She hungrily devoured it, staining the corner of her mouth with mustard. Her face was otherwise clean.

"How have you been able to bathe and take care of yourselves?" Tiffany asked, her curiosity outpacing her manners.

"There's a shelter a few blocks away," the boy said, unoffended, as he spoke around a mouthful of hot dog. "They let us use the shower. We sleep there at night sometimes when they have room, depending on who's working. One wants to go to the cops because my sister is with me instead of our mother, but both of our parents are dead."

"And the cops will split you up," Anna said, "won't they?"

"That's what the good one told us," said the little sister.

Anna knelt down in front of her. "If you stay with me at Avalon, you won't have to worry about that happening ever again."

"Avalon?" the brother asked.

"A...Morgan has a hotel," Tiffany said. "That's where I live, too. I'm Tiffany. Tiffany Sharp. I...I sing. I'll be performing for guests at the hotel soon."

"If my brother shows what he can do with magic, we can live there, too?" the sister asked.

Anna nodded at her and smiled as she tucked a stray curl behind the girl's ear.

"What's the catch?" her brother asked.

Tiffany could see the tension in his jaw as he watched the exchange between Anna and his sister, his expression remaining wary and uncertain.

"There's no catch," Anna said, rising to her feet. "You don't even have to perform if you don't want to. I just get the sense that you wouldn't want something in exchange for nothing. As a show of good faith," she continued after a beat, "I'm going to tell you a secret. My real name is Anna. Morgan is my sister, but she's missing—so I know a thing or two about family."

Now Anna changed her hair from auburn to black. Zaya giggled with delight and clapped her hand. "She can do magic like we can," she said to her brother.

"Only her tricks are just illusions," he said. "Our fire is real." His eyes narrowed as he regarded Anna. "What do you really look like?"

Anna took off her sunglasses. Her pupils grew larger until the brown irises were no longer visible, her hair faded from black to shimmering white, and her skin became translucent, the veins beneath giving the faerie an unearthly blue glow. "One more thing about my sister and I, we come from another world, but our world, like your own, is dying. Our kind didn't always look so strange, but we've had the gift of illusion for as long as I can remember."

"You're beautiful," Zaya said.

She walked to Anna and reached for her hand, tracing the veins beneath her skin. Her brother watched them, looking conflicted.

"That's not all you can do," he said. "I heard your voice in my mind. You told me to stop running. Then you said I didn't need to be afraid anymore."

"You don't," Anna said. "And I apologize for the intrusion. I don't often do that. And I promise I'll never try to hear any thoughts you don't voice aloud." The color returned to her skin and her hair, and she put her sunglasses back on. "The light hurts my eyes," she said.

"I like her, Jax," Zaya said. "I don't want to sleep outside anymore."

Jax sighed. "Alright," he said, reaching for his sister's hand. "But I want to be free to leave at any time. Both of us," he amended.

"Of course." Anna nodded.

Agent Cook drove the company car—a large Ford Escalade—that picked them up from Fremont Street. "She kind of looks like a woman who lived by herself in the mountains near our village," Zaya said when she sat beside her brother in the middle row. "Doesn't she, Jax?" He didn't answer. "She could conjure great storms all by herself," Zaya continued, unfazed. "Even water spouts to keep pirates away."

"I can't do anything like that," Agent Cook said, smiling at Zaya in the rearview window, "but I can turn invisible."

"Not right now, though," Anna said. She sat beside Tiffany in the third row, her hair once again Morgan's fiery shade of auburn. "We don't want to attract any attention to ourselves."

"Before you picked us up, we found out Jax and Zaya learned how to speak English from their parents," Tiffany told Agent Cook, changing the subject. "Isn't that amazing? Apparently, different elementalists have traveled to different parts of this world with plans to emigrate. Others know Spanish or Mandarin, some all three. Maybe even more languages than that."

"We weren't supposed to come here for another year or so," Jax said, sitting next to Zaya in the middle row, "but an asteroid took out our village. We were the only survivors. We traveled for three days before we found a strange cave like the one my parents described."

"A vortex," Agent Baker said. "That's what we call them."

"My parents said our people have traveled to many different worlds," Jax said. "Maybe even yours. Did it have killer plants and slimy green monsters that feed on other beings in their sleep and give them terrible nightmares?"

"Home sweet home," Agent Cook answered with a wry grin.

"Our world had killer plants, too," Zaya said with pride. "And dragons."

"The last dragon disappeared years ago," Jax said. "Something stole an egg and brought it to this world. Travelers passing through our village said it saved both of our worlds after it hatched before moving to someplace new. It could be anywhere now."

"That's true," Anna said. "I think she was lonely. Probably looking for others of her kind."

"I hope she finds them," Zaya said solemnly.

Agent Book pulled up in front of the hotel.

Zaya's eyes widened as a valet in a dark green suit with white satin gloves opened the door and reached for her hand to help her down to the sidewalk.

"Welcome to Avalon," he said, his faded blue eyes twinkling beneath gray eyebrows.

"Avalon," Zaya breathed, gazing up at the opulent hotel in wonder.

Even Jax couldn't hide his awe as Anna led them inside.

"Once we get you two settled into your suite, I'm going to have someone drive us to this wonderful place known as the mall," Anna told Zaya. "It's like a market, but it's much bigger and it's inside, with row after row of stores full of clothing and jewelry and candy and toys, and places to cut your hair and paint your nails…"

"Does Anna have any children of her own?" Jax asked Tiffany in a low voice.

"Not exactly," Tiffany said. "To be honest, I think she's still very much a child herself."

Jax nodded. "But we can trust her?"

"Absolutely," Tiffany said.

chapter twenty-three

Tiffany opted against joining Anna on her excursion to the mall with the elementalist children, but she convinced her to bring Lance, not only for the sake of Jax, but because Lance had more earthly experience than Anna. The faerie queen's enthusiasm could sometimes alarm and overwhelm mere mortals, or even a halfling like Tiffany.

She sat on the sofa eating a half of a turkey sandwich when her phone beeped. Tiffany reached for it and saw a message from Mrs. Mills. Amber was awake. Still not ready for other visitors, but communicating by way of a mini dry erase board Mrs. Mills found at a store across the street from the hospital. *She apologizes for delaying your show and understands if you need to replace her,* said a follow-up message.

Please tell her not to worry, Tiffany messaged back. *I just want her to focus on healing. Everyone sends their love. We miss her very much.* She sat back with a sigh.

Tiffany had worried Anna would want to move the children into Amber's suite, but another suite was available. Still, one day Amber's family would need to come to Avalon to pack up her things. Tiffany knew they intended to bring her home after the hospital discharged her, but she couldn't imagine losing Amber from her work family, let alone replacing her.

If I ever come across Convict Two, she thought, *I'll end him myself.*

The thought startled Tiffany. She made herself finish the first half of her sandwich, then closed the container and put the rest in the fridge. Her phone beeped again when she sat back down on the sofa. Jade this time, inviting her to dinner with Emi and Caitlyn, too. She knew she couldn't avoid them forever. They needed to talk about the future of the show.

"Have you heard anything?" Caitlyn asked as soon as Tiffany sat down beside Jade in their booth at the Wild Hunt. Tiffany was relieved to see everyone had the same idea about dressing more casually in blouses and jeans.

"Good grief," Jade chastised Caitlyn. "Most people say 'hi' first."

"Most people aren't as close as we are," Caitlyn said, unfazed. "The bonds of sisterhood are stronger than the pressure to conform to polite society. Right, Tiff?"

Jade rolled her eyes.

"Right," Tiffany said, hiding a smile. "Amber is awake and in good spirits, according to her parents. They bought her a mini whiteboard to communicate. The doctors still want her to rest for another day or two before she can have other visitors. I think they still need to run some more tests 'n stuff." She trailed off when a server arrived to take their drink orders.

"Is it true she'll never sing again?" Emi asked, dark eyes wide with concern.

"They don't know," Tiffany said. "But I know the plan is that Amber will go home to Florida with her parents. Best case scenario, she will need a lot of time and a lot of speech therapy before she knows what her limitations will be. If any," Tiffany added, even though she didn't want to give the others false hope.

"So, we're having auditions no matter what," Jade said.

"We have to," Tiffany said. "I lost a fire dancer and two aerial gymnasts, though I may have found a replacement for the fire dancer already. Still need to iron out some details with Morgan," she said, giving Caitlyn a meaningful look.

Caitlyn tilted her head, looking puzzled.

"You know, that busker you discovered on Fremont Street?" Tiffany prodded.

"Oh!" Caitlyn's eyes grew wide with understanding.

The server returned with their drinks and a basket of bread with honey almond butter before Tiffany had to explain herself to Jade and Emi. The conversation moved on from Amber and auditions to lighter gossip about other performers and members of the crew.

"I don't suppose the rats have had any new updates to share about Convict Two?" Randy asked Tiffany with a hopeful expression when she returned from the Wild Hunt with a to-go box of steak frites.

"Afraid not," she said, handing him his dinner. "Do you really think he's still on the strip?"

"Probably not," Randy said, "but he couldn't have gone too far with that leg of his. A hairline fracture would be one thing, but you can just make out his femur in the security footage. Not only does a break that severe require medical attention—which he won't be seeking, for obvious reasons—there's also the risk of secondary infections from breaking the skin."

Tiffany paled as she recalled the details of Agent Baker's confrontation with Convict Two. Couldn't have happened to a meaner guy, but serious injuries still made her feel squeamish. "My father was Four," she mused while Randy ate. "You were Six, and the social-climbing imposter was Seven. That leaves One, Three, and Five. Is there a chance any of them are working with Two? Can they help him heal like the faerie that helped Amber?"

"Definitely not," Randy said. "Five is a shapeshifter like me, except a lot less cuddly." He gave Tiffany a sly smile, and she giggled. "The others are not team players. Neither is Convict Two. I've considered the possibility that Convict Two somehow made it as far as Red Rock Canyon. There's a vortex in a small cave. I'm taking a couple agents to check it out tonight. Lance was supposed to come, but Anna had other plans that interrupted his nap. Don't suppose you know anything about that?"

Tiffany brought Randy up to speed on the elementalists while he finished his dinner.

"Pint-size pyromancers," Randy said. "Here in Avalon. Neat."

Tiffany laughed. "The brother is young adult-sized, but I don't think either poses a threat."

"I hope you're right," Randy said, scowling. "Because the only thing that smells worse than a wet dog is a *singed* dog."

Tiffany could tell by the uneasy look in his eyes that Randy was remembering his confrontations with the elementalists in Los Angeles. One had killed her father. Perhaps Tiffany was being too cavalier about the elementalist children, but she couldn't imagine Jax or Zaya hurting anyone.

"Don't mind me." Randy leaned over to kiss Tiffany on the cheek. "I'm just being an old grouch. And maybe it wouldn't hurt to have some extra firepower around here." He smirked.

"They're just kids," Tiffany reminded him.

"As much as I'm loath to admit it," Groucho Manx said after Randy left for the night, "I share the dog's reservations. Nothing but trouble can come from having elementalists in the building. The fact that they're children just means they have less control."

"I dunno if you've noticed," Tiffany said, "but trouble has a way of finding me and mine."

As if to punctuate the sentiment, Gizmo raced across the room in a blur. Tiffany watched his pursuit of nothing with a raised eyebrow. She turned back to Groucho Manx.

"Now there's a cat who's going places," he observed.

chapter twenty-four

"If you're blue and you don't know where to go to," Caitlyn sang in a dirge-like warble the next day, hanging over the edge of a lounge chair. "Why don't you go where Harlem flits?" She rolled from her stomach onto her back. "Putting on the—"

"Like you've ever been to Harlem," Jade scoffed from a neighboring lounge chair.

Emi raised her sunglasses. "Can't you sing something happier? Or at least current?"

"Not without violating copyright," Caitlyn told Emi. She didn't bother reminding Jade she used to live in New York City, including a brief stint at the Apollo Theatre—working as an usher. "Ugh, I'm so bored." She rose from her lounge chair and stretched.

"Enjoy the time off," Emi said. "Once rehearsals start back up, we get maybe a week to ourselves before the show goes live. Then we just have Mondays and Tuesdays off."

"We're lucky," Jade said. "Some shows run every day."

"Yeah, but they probably have different performers so they can rest their voi—"

Caitlyn wandered away from their private cabana to the lazy river. She grabbed the next available empty innertube. At some point she bumped into the innertube of a little girl who squealed with delight as she pinned Caitlyn beneath a waterfall. Despite her young age, maybe eight or nine, she wore designer sunglasses that probably cost more than Caitlyn's whole outfit, and a pink floral bathing suit that offset her dark shoulder-length curls and tawny skin.

"Hey, I know you," Caitlyn said, sitting up straighter. "How do you like Avalon?"

The girl's smile faded. "I don't know *you*."

"Sorry," Caitlyn said. "We haven't met, but I know your brother. I mean, I don't *know* him know him, but we've seen each other." She realized she needed to salvage this interaction fast before the girl screamed for help. "I'm friends with Tiffany."

"You're weird." The girl no longer looking alarmed. "Are you really Tiffany's friend?"

Caitlyn nodded, wincing as a small child operating a large water cannon positioned outside of the lazy river hit her in the face with a maniacal giggle. "I'm in her show," she sputtered, water dripping down her face.

The girl laughed. "My brother's going to be in her show, too."

After a couple floats down the lazy river, Caitlyn visited the snack bar to order four frozen lemonades. The little girl accompanied her back to the cabana.

"This is Zaya," she told Emi and Jade. "Her brother is replacing the fire dancer who dropped out of the show."

"I'm glad you finally found a friend on your own level to hang out with," Jade said.

Caitlyn ignored her.

"Zaya's a pretty name." Emi told the girl. "Where are you from?"

"Around," Zaya answered.

Caitlyn noticed a dark-haired teenager walking down the sidewalk, looking frantic as he scoured the water. His hair wasn't much shorter than the first time she saw him, but Caitlyn would recognize Zaya's brother anywhere. "Over here," she called.

The boy turned. He strode in their direction as soon as he saw Zaya. "I've been looking all over for you," he said, lifting her into his arms. "Thank you," he told Caitlyn, his eyes narrowing in recognition.

Caitlyn shrugged. "Don't mention it."

"Aren't you a little young to perform in Vegas?" Jade asked.

"I'm eighteen," he said, narrowing his eyes. "Aren't you a little old?"

Jade looked almost comical as her jaw dropped in surprise.

"He was busking on Fremont Street." Caitlyn grinned. "He knows how to handle hecklers."

"I'm Emi," Emi said. "That's Jade, and I guess you already know Caitlyn." She held out her hand.

The boy stared at her hand before setting down Zaya to give it a brief shake. "Jax," he said.

"You should come play in the water," Zaya said. "It's so much fun."

"Have fun with the kiddies," Jade told Emi and Caitlyn, sounding bored. "This old lady is heading back inside before I break a hip." She wrapped her towel around her waist like a skirt, then walked away.

"I probably shouldn't have said that," Jax said.

"She'll get over it," Emi told him.

Caitlyn joined Emi later at the hotel buffet. "Jade still nursing a bruised ego?" she asked.

"Nah," Emi said. "She has a date with a dealer from another hotel. Must be nice. Although…" She gave Caitlyn a shy smile. "One of the techies asked me out the other day. His name is Charlie. He helps build the sets. Cute. Big muscles. But I dunno if I wanna mix business and pleasure, you know?"

"Well, his job on the show is just about done," Caitlyn pointed out as she reached for a dinner roll. "So, no more conflict of interest."

"That's true," Emi said. "Maybe I'll message him later."

She led Caitlyn to a quiet wooden table in the corner of the restaurant designed to look like an outdoor eatery with twinkling "stars" overhead and glowing bulbs hanging from fake trees beside every table. A beautiful water fountain lit by color-changing LEDs occupied the center of the large room and played a different song every hour on the hour. Right now, it "danced" in sync to Tiffany's "Stranger to Myself."

"The Lafayette Corporation was in the news again," Emi said after they started eating.

"I don't think the Vegas Ripper story is going away while he's still at large," Caitlyn said.

"Not about him," Emi said. "This creepy guy in New York just got released from prison. You know, the one that was trafficking kids? Supposedly the police mishandled evidence. He insists Morgan le Fay framed him, and now he's talking about running for office."

"Yuck," Caitlyn said. "That's the last thing Morgan needs right now, but at least a campaign should keep him busy and out of trouble. Not that anyone would vote for him."

"Right," Emi said, looking doubtful.

chapter twenty-five

"So, weird question—but what if the assailant wields elemental magic rather than physical weapons?" Bianca asked the self-defense instructor.

"I get that question more often than you'd expect these days," Sensei Laura said. "Honestly, it all comes back to the basics. We practice stepping in and to the side, then striking the opponent's arms. The movement becomes instinctive, and it allows you to evade any number of attacks—be it a fist, a club, or a fireball—and buys you time to consider your next move."

Bianca's brow furrowed. She didn't bother mentioning that some elementalists could zap or incinerate a person with the touch of their hands. The goons working for a certain corrupt millionaire were mere mortals, she reasoned, so she could still benefit from lessons in self-defense. She rolled her shoulders back and practiced the technique against a soft-spoken Taiwanese woman with surprising strength and dexterity.

The class was full of women from all walks of life: different ages, different ethnicities, different tax brackets; a desire to control their own destinies was the only common denominator. After class, Bianca sat down in her beat-up Malibu and checked her phone. An unwelcome news alert caught her attention.

"You have got to be kidding me," she groaned.

. . .

Bianca's own destiny felt even more uncertain now that Emerson Fowler had been released from federal prison. That skeevy lawyer of his managed to overturn his conviction for multiple felony counts of abduction and conspiracy after years of appeals.

Bianca wondered if her brother knew as she walked up the stairs of an apartment complex in downtown Rochester. She hadn't heard from Brian since Christmas. Sometimes he contacted her from a burner phone to catch up and invite her to join him in a mysterious new world inhabited by former victims of Emerson's human trafficking ring.

Perhaps she would take him up on that offer after all.

Bianca knew something was wrong as soon as she approached the door to her apartment and saw that it was ajar. She considered calling the police but decided against it, pushing the door open instead. Bianca gasped, then slapped her hand over her mouth as she stepped inside. Her apartment had been ransacked. The TV still sat in the built-in entertainment center of the small living room, but her laptop was gone from the kitchen counter.

Definitely not a run-of-the-mill thief. One of Emerson's goons, perhaps?

What if they were still there?

The door to the bedroom from the living room was wide open. If anyone was still here, they'd have to be hiding in her bathroom. Bianca held her breath and listened. Nothing. She steeled herself as she walked into the bedroom. The bed had been stripped, the sheets piled on the floor. All the drawers of her dresser and nightstand were still open, the contents spilling everywhere. What a mess.

Bianca still felt afraid, but now she felt a growing flame of anger as well. It burned in her chest and rose up her neck and face. Resolute, Bianca forced herself to walk to the bathroom. It was less of a mess than the bedroom, but the intruder had clearly looked through her medicine cabinet and under the sink. Nobody stood behind the shower curtain.

Bianca breathed a sigh of relief. She walked out of the bedroom, across the living room, and into the kitchen. Bianca once again considered calling the cops as she stared at the empty space where her laptop had sat on the counter. With her luck, they'd mistake her for the intruder.

Bianca decided to call her old friend Lance instead. She knew he'd moved from Buffalo to Las Vegas almost a year ago, but his number remained the same.

Someone walked into the apartment and released a low whistle before Bianca made the call. A blond man in a pale pink polo shirt and khakis stood before her. She reached behind herself to open the cutlery drawer and hoped whatever she grabbed would work as a weapon. "I'll cut you," she said as she stepped out of the kitchen.

The man looked down at her hand. "With a butter knife?"

Bianca groaned inwardly. Aloud, she said, "It won't be quick, but it will be painful."

The man considered, grimacing. Instead of retreating, he closed the front door behind him and took a few steps toward Bianca, showing his palms. "I'm not the one who broke into your apartment," he said. "Brian asked me to come."

"Brian?" Bianca raised an eyebrow. "Why didn't he come himself?"

"He only just heard about Emerson Fowler's release, but he was attending to some matters in Las Vegas. His flight doesn't even leave until midnight," he said. "I was the closest, well, operative, I guess you can say. We met when I was a youth counselor at a shelter in Pennsylvania."

"You haven't told me anything that Emerson's people couldn't make up themselves," Bianca said. "How do I know you aren't one of his goons?"

"Do I look like an enforcer?"

Bianca considered. The man was tall and lean, fit, but not brutish in the slightest. Still, one thing she'd learned from self-defense is that skill can win over brute force. "You look like you could be Emerson's golf caddy," she said, testing him.

He gave a rueful laugh and ran a hand through his wavy blond hair, which was just tousled enough to be fashionable without looking unkempt. Something about that annoyed Bianca, but she felt her resolve weakening. This guy could tell her he was a former eagle scout who spent his weekends reading to old people at rest homes, and she'd believe it.

Bianca put away the butter knife. "So, what now?"

"I booked a room at the hotel nearest to Rochester International. It's a single, but there's a sleeper sofa," the man said. "Brian would kill me if anything happened to you before he arrived."

"I don't even know your name," Bianca said.

"I'm sorry," he said. "It's Kyle."

"You're sorry your name is Kyle?" Bianca smirked. "I've heard worse."

"No," Kyle laughed. "I'm sorry I asked you to spend the night with me before I even introduced myself."

Bianca allowed herself to crack a genuine smile in return. "I'm an old-fashioned girl," she told him. "You need to buy me dinner first." She looked around her wrecked apartment and sighed. "Honestly, the sooner we get out of here, the better."

"So, how long have you known Brian?"

Bianca sat across from Kyle at a twenty-four-hour diner near the hotel. She still wore the loose tank top and leggings she wore to her self-defense class, but she had put on a hoodie and packed a suitcase with a few days' worth of clothing and underwear in the trunk of his car.

"About five years," Kyle said. "And I've known about other worlds for longer than that," he added under his breath after the server dropped off a plate of buttermilk waffles for Kyle, and a burger and fries for Bianca.

"Do you recruit kids to move to Anna's world or something?" Bianca asked.

"No," Kyle said, "but I found out about it the same way Brian did. One of our regulars disappeared. Only twelve or thirteen years old, but he was living on the street after his parents kicked him out. The usual reason." A note of bitterness entered Kyle's otherwise friendly voice. "I thought maybe his parents had a change of heart, but my trail led me to an abandoned shack the cult members were meeting in. That's where I met Anna. I've been a scout ever since. Usually, I stick around here to earn money and gather supplies for the other world."

As he talked, Bianca began to understand why Brian trusted him. Not just because she could tell she wasn't his type, but because he was a sincere stand-up guy trying his best to help others in a messed-up world stacked against most kids in a hundred different ways. She liked him. And that made her worried for him.

"What happens next? After Brian gets here."

"I drive back to Pennsylvania," Kyle said. "I don't think anyone saw me. Whoever ransacked your apartment was long gone before either of us arrived. I'm not really on Emerson Fowler's radar. Black Anna. Her sister.

You. That filmmaker-turned-TV-personality. That's who we expect him to target."

D'Andre. Bianca hadn't even thought about him in forever, she realized with a pang of guilt. They didn't have a falling-out. They just lost touch after she abandoned their planned documentary about her investigation. But now D'Andre was living in Hollywood. He had worked his way up from hosting his own show on social media to taking over *Entertainment Daily*. Surely, he had moved into one of those swanky gated communities with security guards on duty twenty-four seven.

Then again, didn't that pop star get taken hostage in her own home?

And she was half-Fae!

Bianca must have looked worried because Kyle told her, "Brian already reached out to him, too. He didn't seem all that worried. After all, he has connections you don't."

"Absolutely not," Bianca told Brian the next morning. He had arrived from the airport in a dark gray hoodie and baggy jeans with bloodshot eyes and a strained smile. Kyle left to return to Pennsylvania shortly thereafter.

"Oh, come on," Brian said. "I know you've at least thought about coming with me."

"No, I have not," Bianca lied, folding her arms across her chest.

"Bianca..." Brian made his puppy dog eyes at her as if she'd be swayed.

"No, Brian, I gave it a lot of thought last night, and I don't think Emerson plans to kill me," Bianca said.

"What about your apartment?"

"He probably just sent someone to make sure I didn't have any incriminating evidence left to use against him," Bianca said. "If he wanted me dead, the person responsible would have waited for me to come home to finish the job. No, he can't risk something happening to me. Not if he plans to run for office."

"What's he gonna run for, anyway?" Brian scoffed. "County dipshit?"

"Sounds like he's thinking bigger than local politics," Bianca said. "Not like the bar's all that high anymore."

"Just one more reason to leave this crazy-ass world behind," Brian said.

chapter twenty-six

B rian left the hotel feeling exasperated. Bianca had agreed that she couldn't stay there anymore, not at that apartment and not in Rochester, maybe not even New York at all. Her landlord had reached out, frantic after discovering the state of the apartment. He acquiesced to terminating the lease over the phone but made it clear Bianca would not be getting her security deposit back. No shocker there.

"Two hundred bucks is worth not seeing that mess again," Bianca had said. "Think they need social workers in Pennsylvania?"

Brian didn't think Pennsylvania was far enough either, but he asked Kyle to look into job opportunities for Bianca once he made it home.

While Kyle drove to Pennsylvania, Brian drove to Bianca's apartment to pack up the rest of her things. One nice thing about growing up in foster care was that Brian and Bianca learned to limit their physical possessions. Most of the furniture came with the apartment, so Brian only needed a couple suitcases to pack up clothing, bedding, and a few precious mementos—a small jewelry box with a black ballerina inside, a well-loved teddy bear with a blue bow tie, and a plush blanket. Brian had a teddy bear and blanket of his own, gifts from their mother.

By the time Brian returned to the hotel parking lot, Kyle had messaged him. *Saw a protest happening downtown. A lot of Emerson Fowler's victims came from a shelter near here. Anything in Rochester?*

Not that I saw, Brian messaged back, *but Bianca's apartment is in a quieter neighborhood.*

"Emerson Fowler's holding a press conference outside his home in twenty minutes," Bianca told Brian when he came inside. "I'm not sure I can stomach seeing his smug face on TV." She took one of the suitcases from his outstretched hand and set it down on the coffee table. "Oh Brian, you even packed Blueberry for me." Bianca hugged the stuffed bear to her chest.

"I still got my Blackberry," Brian told her. "But Simone calls him Squinty McStank-Eye because one of his eyes fell off and the only thing she had to replace it was a little button, so now he just looks all grizzled and grouchy."

"I suppose Blueberry has seen better days himself," Bianca said. "How *is* Simone? You living together now?"

Brian knew from her pointed tone she wasn't making casual conversation. "I'd like to make things official," he said, "but we've been so busy, what with trying to build a functional society in a strange new world. Marriage hasn't topped our to-do list, and somehow bringing her with me to get hitched in Vegas didn't seem like the right vibe."

"I'm just messing with you," Bianca said. "It sounds like you have a good thing going."

"I know a lot of great hardworking guys looking to get a good thing going for themselves," Brian ventured. "Women, too. I got the sense it wasn't like that with you and D'Andre, but I didn't know if it was him specifically, or dudes in general. No judgment," he added quickly.

"Romance is even less of a priority for me," Bianca said. "I think I'd rather just be the eccentric auntie that travels the world and spoils her nieces and nephews. But maybe without the yappy purse dog. Even that's too much of a commitment for me."

"Nieces and neph—" " Brian felt queasy. "You know what? Forget I brought it up."

Despite Bianca's reservations, they tuned into Emerson Fowler's press conference. The first thing Brian noticed was the pale blond woman of indeterminate age standing at his side. She had frosty pink lips and wore her hair pulled back in a chignon.

"I don't know how I would have survived my time in federal prison had this wonderful woman not reached out to me," Emerson Fowler boasted, looking less like he'd been released from prison and more like he just came home from vacation to an exotic tropical locale somewhere. Brian doubted the prison guards had him doing hard labor in the sun; makeup seemed more likely.

"Someone knows how to blend," Bianca said, apparently drawing a similar conclusion.

"When it became apparent my former lawyer was not up to the task of representing me in court to appeal the outlandish charges filed against me and my unjust imprisonment, Veronica Highmore offered her services pro bono." Emerson Fowler turned to smile at her. "Neither of us expected romance to blossom, but here we are. I'm proud to have Veronica at my side as I rebuild my life and consider a run for Congress."

"Doesn't that present an ethical dilemma?" a reporter asked off camera.

"I don't see how," Emerson said. "Veronica has a mutual interest in my future endeavors as both my legal representation and future wife. There's no conflict here." He chuckled. "I think the real ethical dilemma is how I came to find myself falsely imprisoned in the first place, wouldn't you agree?" he asked his lawyer.

"I think it's a real travesty of justice that the state of New York allowed this witch hunt against Emerson while an actual witch who is neither a citizen of the country nor the planet runs a corrupt transgalactic enterprise." The camera zoomed in for a closeup of Veronica Highmore's unlined face. Her blue eyes flashed as she continued speaking. "Morgan le Fay, not Emerson Fowler, is the real threat to the people of this great nation, and our children in particular."

"Oh, so that's how it's gonna be?" Brian said, staring at the screen.

"What else did you expect from a guy like Emerson Fowler?" Bianca reached for the remote and turned off the TV. "I have a bad feeling those two are about to become a big headache for more than just you and me."

"My offer still stands," Brian said. "You don't have to stay and watch the shit show."

Bianca threw Blueberry at his head. Brian ducked.

chapter twenty-seven

L ance contacted Tiffany and Randy for an emergency meeting with Anna. They hoped it had nothing to do with Randy's first trip through the vortex in Red Rock Cavern. He had found no sign of Convict Two but planned to try again tonight. Now he was heading down to Anna's office instead of sleeping.

"What's going on?" Tiffany asked as Lance led them into Anna's living quarters instead of her office.

"Have you seen the press conference?" Anna sat on a fluffy cream blanket in the middle of a genuine black leather couch, wearing a black and white pinstripe pencil skirt and matching jacket over a silk crimson blouse. Her eyes were wide.

"What press conference?" Randy and Tiffany looked at each other, perplexed.

"Have a seat," Anna said, patting the couch. "I'll show you."

Randy and Tiffany sat on either side of Anna. Lance remained standing, his muscular arms folded over his chest as he stared at a large flatscreen television nestled in a recessed wall across from the couch.

Anna pressed a button on the remote. Tiffany read more news than she watched, but she recognized the man on the screen as Emerson Fowler. There was also something familiar about the blond woman standing beside him, but she couldn't place her. After Emerson introduced the woman, she gave an impassioned speech attacking Morgan le Fay.

"I guess Emerson Fowler's fancy new lawyer didn't get the memo about Morgan's disappearance," Randy said.

"I think that *is* Morgan," Tiffany said. "What is she doing?"

"It's Vivienne," Lance said, "cosplaying as one of those scary Moms for Liberty-types."

"I don't love that for her," Anna said as she watched her sister on the screen.

"The excessive mascara and eyeliner or the fiery rhetoric?" Lance asked.

"Either," Anna said. After a beat, "Lance—what are we going to do?"

"Not much we *can* do," Lance said. "Not until we know what we're up against. If it was just Emerson Fowler, I'd be inclined to dismiss it as nothing but bluster and preemptive campaigning, but now that Vivienne is involved, who knows what her real intentions are. We should probably shore up your legal defenses in case she tries to attack you—or rather, Morgan—through the courts."

They returned their attention to the television. Now Emerson and Veronica were insinuating Morgan le Fay was behind the killings by the Vegas Ripper. "Sacrificing children attracted too much attention," Veronica was saying, "so Morgan le Fay took a calculated risk that women of the night would inspire less public sympathy. Don't get me wrong. I don't approve of their work, but only God can judge the trespasses of these poor young women."

"They aren't even prostitutes," Tiffany yelled at the television. "Nobody calls them women of the night anymore, anyway."

"If you're going to bring back the classics," Lance said, "why stop at fear and xenophobia?"

After that horrifying press conference, Tiffany felt thrilled to receive some good news for a refreshing change. Mrs. Mills reached out while Randy tried to salvage the rest of his nap. *Amber is ready for visitors*, the message read. *Taking it easy for tonight. She just wants to see you. More friends can visit tomorrow.*

Tiffany changed out of her sweats into a green tank top and jeans. She went downstairs to the hotel gift shop named "Fanciful Notions and

Potions." There she selected a get-well card with shimmering butterflies, a plush golden retriever puppy with big glittery eyes, and a bouquet of pink stargazer lilies and yellow roses. Tiffany considered a box of gourmet chocolates—Amber's sweet tooth rivaled Caitlyn's—but she realized Amber may not be ready to enjoy the gift.

A bottle of wine didn't seem appropriate either, but Tiffany accepted a free sample from an enthusiastic sommelier in a velvet green mini-dress. "Not to be nosy," the sommelier said, "but is all that stuff for Amber Mills? I didn't know her personally, but I'm so glad she's going to make it. Everyone at Avalon is pulling for her."

"I'll give her your regards," Tiffany said with a wan smile.

After she assured the sommelier and the store clerk that her show would still be opening in September, Tiffany left the gift shop. She requested a ride to the hospital from the front desk and went outside to wait.

Mrs. Mills embraced Tiffany when she arrived at the hospital. "Adam took Sienna out to eat," she said. "She threatened a hunger strike if she had to go one more day without real French fries from a quality dining establishment."

"Fast food?" Tiffany grinned.

"Fast food," Mrs. Mills confirmed. "In fairness, the only edible food in the hospital cafeteria is the five layer chocolate cake. I could use a break from this place myself." She sighed. "Maybe tomorrow. Oh, you probably think I'm just awful complaining about trivialities after I almost lost my daughter."

"No," Tiffany said, "I think the lighting would drive anyone bonkers after a few days."

"Let's go see Amber," Mrs. Mills said. "She can't wait to see you."

It took all of Tiffany's force of will not to cry out when she saw Amber laying in the hospital bed, her skin pale and washed out, her neck heavily bandaged. Despite her condition, Amber smiled when she saw Tiffany. She clapped as Tiffany pulled her gifts out of a large gift bag and arranged them on the counter. She set a vase holding the stargazer lilies and roses beside another vase with pink roses and white baby's breath flowers.

Amber wrote something on a white board. It read: *you didn't have to do all that.* She punctuated the sentiment with a magnet resembling a blushing emoji.

"You're lucky I didn't buy out the whole store," Tiffany told her. "I had such a hard time deciding what to get for you."

Favorite dog. Favorite colors. You did good.

"I'll leave you two girls alone to catch up," Mrs. Mills said, standing behind Tiffany. "That chocolate cake is calling to me." Amber pouted. "Sorry," Mrs. Mills told Amber. "Just as soon as the doctors give us the go-ahead, you can have all the chocolate you want."

"How do you feel?" Tiffany asked after Mrs. Mills left. "Really?"

Like I could use a hug, Amber wrote on her white board. *I think my family is afraid I'll break if they touch me.*

Tiffany walked to the bed. She leaned over to give Amber a hug, taking care not to brush against her neck injury.

Thank you, Amber mouthed. On her white board, she wrote: *the Vegas Ripper is one of the Fae, isn't he?*

Tiffany pressed her lips together. She nodded.

Were the people who saved me Fae?

Tiffany nodded again.

Wild.

Amber offered Tiffany a wry grin.

Tiffany caught her up on the events of the past few days. She wished she had better news to offer regarding the Vegas Ripper's whereabouts, and she didn't want to talk about the show at all, but Amber remained in good spirits. She listened with interest as Tiffany told her about the elementalist children and brought her up to speed on other strange visitors to their world.

Any other weird stuff I should know about?

"I can talk to animals now," Tiffany said.

I was being serious.

"So am I."

. . .

Tiffany left the hospital feeling better about holding auditions in less than a week. Amber had admitted to feeling homesick even before the attack. She'd already planned to take a break from performing after the residency ended. The attack just forced her to readjust her plans by a year. Besides, Amber had all these new insights to process.

Who wouldn't feel ready to hide from reality in suburbia if reality now included not only murderous Fae, but elementalists and shapeshifters of questionable intent?

Tiffany longed for a return to normalcy herself, but she had no choice but to move that particular goalpost. *A cabin in the woods*, she remembered Randy once saying, *one day when you've had enough of performing and crazy faerie business, we're going to move to a cabin in the woods to live the rest of our days in peace. If not here, then whatever world will have us.*

It was a nice dream, Tiffany thought as she got ready for bed, but somehow, she doubted it would ever be anything more than that. Especially now that Player Two—no, Player Three—had entered the game.

Just what did Vivienne think she was doing?

And where was Morgan?

chapter twenty-eight

Caitlyn didn't know who appointed her Zaya's unofficial babysitter except for maybe Zaya herself, but she'd spent most of yesterday entertaining a hyperactive goblin with an even bigger appetite than she she had. Today threatened to be a repeat of yesterday.

"Where's Jax?" she asked when Zaya knocked on her door sometime after eight. Eight on a weekend, no less. Well, okay. Wednesday was technically not a weekend, but it may as well have been for Caitlyn until rehearsals started back up.

"He discovered this magical place called a fitness center," Zaya said, her voice dripping with more sarcasm than any nine-year-old child should possess, no matter their home planet. "Now he'd rather lift weights than play with me. I think he has a crush on the grumpy old lady."

"The grumpy old...do you mean Jade?" Caitlyn grimaced. "She's like my age."

Zaya giggled. "I know. I just like the faces she makes when she's annoyed. They're funny."

Caitlyn couldn't argue with her there. "Well, what about Morgan?"

"She has a job." Zaya rolled her eyes.

"*I* have a job!"

"Not right now, you don't."

"You should try making friends with kids your own age," Caitlyn said, exasperated. "I've seen all sorts of kids at the pool and in the arcade."

"They all have families," Zaya said. Her eyes went wide and shiny with unshed tears, and her lower lip jutted out. That did it.

"Have you eaten breakfast yet?"

Caitlyn reached for a hoodie to put on over her tank top. She still wore the clothes she slept in and couldn't be bothered to trade in her flannel boxers for a pair of pants.

Zaya twirled happily in her pale blue sundress. "Can we go back to the buffet?"

After missing out on a trip to the hospital with Emi and Jade to take Zaya out to the pool after breakfast and then learning just how many chicken nuggets a nine-year-old girl could consume between shooting hoops in the arcade, Caitlyn was ready to pull her hair out. She had the front desk page for Jax to retrieve his sister.

"We're auditioning people next week, and I'm not going to have time to run after your sister once rehearsals start back up," Caitlyn told him in an empty alcove near the elevators.

Jax looked stunned. "I thought you were hanging out in the suite," he said to Zaya. "There's a TV and the thing with all the games and Anna bought all those books. She said she would get someone to help you learn how to read. And an icebox full of food."

"I get bored," Zaya told him.

"Well, you can't make that everyone else's problem," Jax said. "I'm sorry," he told Caitlyn. "Thank you for looking after my sister."

"I don't mind if it's a sometimes thing," Caitlyn said, softening her tone. "Wait a minute. Who's Anna? Did you mean Morgan?"

"Right. Morgan," Jax said, looking even more dismayed than he already did.

"Jax is just dumb sometimes," Zaya said.

"Okay, well, I have things I need to take care of," Caitlyn said. "Maybe we can hang out at the pool tomorrow," she told Zaya. "But I'll plan it with your brother first. You know how to use the phone in the room, right?"

Jax nodded. "It's almost dinnertime," he said to Zaya. "You hungry?"

"I want to eat a burger," Zaya told him. "A big one. Not the little kid burger."

Caitlyn shook her head in awe as she watched Zaya drag her brother away.

Tiffany messaged Caitlyn just as she collapsed on the sofa in her suite.

Have you been able to visit Amber yet? I was going to stop by the hospital and grab some food on the way back. Wanna come with?

OMG yes! Caitlyn messaged back. *I spent all day with Zaya. That kid is crazy.*

Caitlyn took a quick shower and changed into a gray crop top and jeans. She was still brushing the tangles out of her damp hair when Tiffany arrived. "The strangest thing happened when I talked to Jax today," she said. "He called Morgan by the wrong name."

"It's been a crazy few days." Tiffany avoided Caitlyn's gaze as she tidied up her toiletries. "He's probably just confused. Besides, weren't you supposed to put away your detective cap?"

"I know Anna's a common name," Caitlyn continued, "but I don't know any here."

"Sometimes Morgan went by Morgana," Tiffany said, looking tense. "Maybe she gave him that name instead. It's not a big leap to go from Morgana to Anna."

"Something's up, I can tell," Caitlyn persisted. "Besides, the Morgan I met here and the Morgan I met way back when during *Dracula* seem very different. I never said anything before because I thought I was just imagining things, but then Jax called her by the wrong name, and now you're acting all weird."

Tiffany sighed. "Sometimes I think you're in your own little world, but other times your intuition rivals even the Fae. Anna is Morgan's little sister. I've never even met the real Morgan le Fay. She's been missing for a while now."

Caitlyn's eyes lit up. "And Anna's been pretending to be Morgan this whole time so she can keep the Lafayette Corporation running!"

"Exactly." Tiffany watched as Caitlyn put down her detangling comb and reached for a scrunchie to pull back her hair. "So, it's not something we want getting out. Not with everything else that's been going wrong."

"Understood." Caitlyn met her gaze in the mirror. "Your secret's safe with me."

"Mr. and Mrs. Mills went out to eat at a real restaurant," a receptionist told Tiffany and Caitlyn when they signed in. "The other daughter insisted. I think she wants a break from her parents flittering about, if you ask me."

A teenage girl in headphones sat in the waiting room reading a book. "That's Amber's sister, Sienna," Tiffany told Caitlyn. "She doesn't like my music."

"Your cover of 'Fairytale' was better than I expected," Sienna said without looking up from her book. "Fire and Ash is one of my favorite bands."

Tiffany gave Caitlyn a sheepish look before turning to smile at Sienna. "Is that who you're listening to, now?"

"Nah," Sienna answered. "Reading along with an audiobook." She held up a paperback of what appeared to be a paranormal romance called *Love Bites*. "My parents don't let me listen to music with my headphones because I turn the volume up too loud, and they're worried I'll damage my ears. Especially when Makayla Watson screams."

"I'm seeing the band again soon," Tiffany told her. "I can get their autographs for you, if you'd like."

"Cool," Sienna said, returning her attention to her book.

"I like her," Tiffany said to Caitlyn. "Reminds me of my sisters. I can't believe Lily goes to Julliard in a month. Time flies."

A nurse approached them. "Amber's ready for more guests," she said. "Try to keep it brief. She's been a very popular lady today."

"Go on," Tiffany told Caitlyn. "I'm gonna hang out here with my girl, Sienna."

Caitlyn pushed aside her apprehension as she walked into the room. One moment she was standing in a sparse hallway with that icky faint greenish light she remembered from when her mother was ill; the next she found herself lost in a sea of fragrant flowers, shiny balloons, and assorted stuffed animals—including a bear as tall as her in the corner of the room. She looked down at the card she had painstakingly selected for Amber, then added it to a pile of cards she spotted on the counter.

Amber was gazing at her from the bed with an amused expression. She looked good—pale despite the addition of modest blush, but alert. Someone had curled her long blond hair for visitors. She wore it over her shoulders, but the bandages on her neck were hard to disguise, if that was the intent.

"I'm sorry about your neck," Caitlyn said, then winced. That was lame.

Amber scrawled something on her whiteboard and held it up.

It's a good thing I've always been a better dancer than a singer, Caitlyn read. She felt her eyes fill with tears, both from the guilt gnawing away at her stomach and the pang in her heart for Amber.

"I should have left the theater when you asked me to," Caitlyn said.

I should have waited for the next elevator, Amber wrote. Then she pressed her lips together in determination and added more: *maybe it wouldn't have mattered. If the Ripper chooses his victims in advance, he would have gotten me alone at one point or another.* She held up a finger and erased her board to make room. *Or maybe he would have targeted a different victim and they wouldn't have been as lucky.*

"Lucky?" Caitlyn blurted out.

It's not every day you cheat death, Amber wrote. *Or get saved by a handsome stranger from another world.* More erasing, then writing. *The last thing I saw were the most beautiful blue eyes. I thought for sure he was an angel until I woke up in a hospital instead of heaven.*

Huh, Caitlyn thought. She didn't think Agent Baker ever took his sunglasses off. She felt an odd twinge of envy for someone without a gaping neck wound.

Speaking of handsome, check out the bear, Amber now wrote, apparently anxious to change the subject. *Turns out Miguel has a crush on me.* She smiled. Her eyes grew big and her smile widened as she erased, then wrote: *I also got a very sweet card and flowers from that weird stagehand Becky. Not my usual type, but she's cute. Shame I'm leaving town once I'm better.*

"I wish you could stay," Caitlyn said. "The show won't be the same without you."

Tiffany's the star. We can't ride her coattails forever.

Oof. Caitlyn tried not to show it, but that hurt.

I just mean I'm ready for a new chapter in life, preferably with less blood and terror. Amber made a look of mock horror as she held up the white board.

Caitlyn mustered a smile. "Maybe a romance if Miguel can visit you in Florida. Or Becky. Both if you're feeling adventurous!"

Amber wheezed with apparent laughter, then winced.

"Sorry."

Stay safe, Cat. I mean it. Getting a little tired.

Amber set down the white board and held out her arms. Caitlyn gave her a light hug. When she pulled away, Amber used a button on the bedside remote to dim the lights. She gestured at a smaller stuffed bear on the counter. Caitlyn handed it to her. Amber hugged it tight against her chest and closed her eyes.

Caitlyn didn't have much of an appetite when she left the hospital with Tiffany. Nick sent a message while she was getting ready to call it an early night, lest Zaya show up unannounced again in the morning.

I know you're supposed to wait a few days before texting back, but I couldn't help myself.

Caitlyn frowned, then scrolled back through their messages. *You texted last,* she typed back, *but I don't think there's a set amount of time to wait.*

Fair point, Nick replied. *I was hoping you wouldn't catch that.*

Caitlyn started brushing her teeth while dots appeared and disappeared on her phone. She had spit, rinsed, and cleaned the sink by the time Nick completed his message. That long just to ask what she was doing this weekend?

Against her better judgment, if such a thing even existed, Caitlyn replied, *what do you have in mind?*

Working Friday and Saturday night but free on Sunday. I can meet you there around noon and we can wing it from there.

Caitlyn figured she couldn't get in too much trouble during the day, so she agreed.

chapter twenty-nine

To Caitlyn's pleasant surprise, Zaya let her sleep on Thursday morning. She didn't see the girl until after lunch, when Caitlyn offered to take her out to the pool for a few hours. Then Caitlyn met Emi and Jade for a kid-free dinner. Friday and Saturday passed largely the same, except she stayed out late to dance at the Grotto.

Caitlyn forgot all about her date with Nick until he messaged her shortly before noon to say he would be there soon. She swore and climbed out of bed to see if she could do something about her hair. Her stubborn eyeliner had survived washing last night and this morning, so she just had to curl her lashes and apply a light coat of mascara. She was just putting away her lip gloss wand when someone knocked on the door.

Nick took one look at her when she opened the door and bit his lip on a smile.

"I…just need another minute to get dressed," Caitlyn told him, realizing she hadn't changed out of her thin tank top and sleep shorts. She left him in the living room and closed the bedroom door behind her. She leaned back against it, taking a few deep breaths before walking to the closet to pick out a more supportive burgundy tank top, jeans, and sporty ballet flats.

"Late night?" Nick asked when she returned to the living room.

"After hours at the Grotto," Caitlyn said. "They had a guest DJ from Europe. I'll be fine once I get some breakf…err, lunch in me."

"I know a place if you don't mind a short drive," Nick said. "You might wanna grab your suit and some sunblock before we go." He returned her inquisitive look with a mysterious smile.

Nick led Caitlyn through the parking lot. He stopped beside a red Corvette convertible. It was an older model but well-kept. "High school graduation present from my parents," he said, "but it almost never left their garage until I moved west. Probably too hot to put the top down today. We're gonna want the AC."

"That's okay," Caitlyn said, remembering the mess Tiffany's BMW convertible always made of her hair when she drove with the top down. Nick opened the passenger side door and she sat down, immediately grateful she wore jeans instead of shorts or a skirt as she felt the heat of the cream-colored leather seats through her clothes.

"Careful when you buckle," Nick said. "Actually, let me get that for you." He leaned over to fasten her seat belt, taking almost exaggerated care not to brush against her body. "Fried my hand the other day," Nick explained when he sat down in the driver's seat. He held up his hand to show Caitlyn a healing burn on his index finger. "Gonna give the car a few minutes to cool down before I even think of touching the steering wheel."

"Where are we going?" Caitlyn asked after Nick had been driving for a few minutes. Unlike her, he was wearing shorts, but they were loose cargo shorts that stopped just below the knee. She'd never seen him dressed so casually before.

"I thought we could both use a break from the strip," he said. "Just be patient."

Patience was not a virtue Caitlyn possessed, but she was ninety-nine-point nine percent sure Nick wasn't taking her somewhere to kill her, so she tried to sit back and enjoy the desert scenery. After another half hour or so, they arrived at what appeared to be a marina.

"Have you ever been to Lake Mead before?" Nick asked.

Caitlyn shook her head.

"Dan felt like taking the boat out today," Nick said. "He'll be here in about an hour or so. Plenty of time for us to grab lunch."

After Nick parked his car, he led Tiffany to a dock in front of what appeared to be a floating restaurant. Once they were inside, a host led them to a table next to a picture window overlooking the lake and the mountains that surrounded it.

"They have the best milkshakes," Nick told Tiffany.

As they ate lunch, Nick entertained Tiffany with more stories about his family. His father blamed Nick for some of his gray hairs, but Nick's sister Chloe for most. "That's what happens when you spoil the baby," Nick said. "Chloe never heard the word 'no' growing up. That's why she doesn't know what signs like 'no speeding' and 'no passing zone' mean. She just breezes right past the 'no' and does whatever else the sign says."

On the flipside, his older brother Dimitri was the golden child who could do no wrong. Literally. "He didn't even participate in his senior ditch day," Nick said. "Can you imagine that guy keeping it a secret when you stay out too late? Unless you're Chloe, of course. For her, he'd move mountains."

Caitlyn shrugged. She would have been the oldest if her parents had any other children. And if her experience with Zaya was any indication, she would have been wrapped around that kid's finger, just like Dimitri with Chloe. Her parents tried for a second child. When it didn't work, that's when they found out about her mother's cancer. She hadn't planned on sharing such a heavy story with Nick so soon, but it poured out of her.

Nick didn't say anything when she finished. Just reached for her hand and held it until a server interrupted the moment by inquiring about dessert.

"I don't think I could eat another bite after that milkshake," Caitlyn said.

After lunch, they found Dan preparing an impressive white cabin cruiser with metallic blue accents at the boat launch. Like Nick, he came from a wealthy family. Unlike Nick, he was a med student working as a bartender to help pay tuition. He was also taller and beefier, with dirty blond hair, tanned skin, and a friendly smile.

His girlfriend Sadie was so short that Caitlyn found the physical logistics of their relationship mindboggling. Nick helped Dan finish while Caitlyn made awkward small talk with his girlfriend. Sadie, Caitlyn soon learned, was an unabashed Sharpie. The concert tee over her swimsuit was a dead giveaway. Caitlyn was just about to evade a question regarding Tiffany's love life when Dan announced they were ready to depart.

"Sunblock first, then life jacket," Nick told Caitlyn after she changed in the cabin. "Need a hand?" He held the tube in one hand.

"Are you just using this as an excuse to touch me?" she teased.

Nick merely smiled.

"Do you like to fish?" Dan asked Caitlyn. His inquiry provided a welcome distraction from Nick's hand on her back and shoulders as he worked the sunblock into her skin.

"No, but I like to eat fish so I'm grateful for people who do," Caitlyn said.

"Neither does Nick," Dan said, sounding disappointed.

"That just means more for you, big guy."

Caitlyn enjoyed sitting back as the boat sped along the water and the wind, hot as it was, blew her hair away from her face. Nick coaxed her into the water when Dan found a spot he wanted to stop to fish.

"Do you ski?" Sadie asked, swimming out to join them as they tread water.

"Sorta. I've only ever taken the scenic route." Nick smirked. "Underwater," he clarified when Sadie and Caitlyn exchanged puzzled looks. "I've never mastered the mechanics of leaning back in one direction when a boat is driving in the other."

Sadie turned back to Caitlyn. "Does Tiffany ski? You can invite her to join us sometime."

"Hey Sadie, does Dan still have that innertube? Maybe Caitlyn would like to go for a ride."

Caitlyn gave Nick a grateful smile over Sadie's shoulder. Her gratitude was short-lived as she soon found herself screaming uselessly into the wind. She tried to hold on tight to the inner tube handles while Dan towed her at what felt like break-neck speeds until she hit an especially big bump and fell out.

"How fast were you going?" she asked once she was safely back in the boat.

"Only about thirty miles per hour," Dan said. "Have fun?"

"So *much* fun," she lied through gritted teeth.

. . .

"I hope that wasn't too terribly painful," Nick said when they returned to shore hours later. He opened the passenger-side door for Caitlyn.

"I didn't hit the water that hard," she told him.

"I meant dealing with Sadie," Nick said. He drove for about twenty minutes before pulling into the parking lot of a Mexican restaurant overlooking the city of Las Vegas. "If you think this is nice," Nick said after the host led them to their seats, "wait until sunset."

"I should probably check a mirror, for all the good it'll do," said Caitlyn. "I probably look like a drowned rat."

"Rats are actually pretty cute if you can get past the tail," Nick said. "I heard so many horror stories about sewer rats in New York City before I moved there. Nobody prepares you for how adorable they are. Big, but adorable. Maybe not so much the ones who invaded during opening night of *Dracula*, though. Those things were like something out of a nightmare."

The server came to take their drink orders before Caitlyn could tell Nick those "rats" were from another world entirely.

"The Cadillac margarita and the Cosmo are both great," Nick told Caitlyn. "I'm driving, so I'll just have whatever lemon lime soda you offer these days," he said to the server. They shared chips with salsa before their meals and churros for dessert.

When the check came, Caitlyn grabbed it before Nick. "You've already fed me twice," she said. "And working for Tiffany is not unlike winning the jackpot."

"If you insist," Nick said, unoffended.

"I could drop you off at your hotel." Nick said when they returned to the strip, "but I'm not quite ready to end the date." They walked down the strip instead, catching up on everything happening in their lives since *Dracula* closed—a challenge for Caitlyn, who didn't want to provide too many details about Tiffany's personal life beyond what the media already revealed. She mostly talked about the world tour, even her brief fling with the guitarist of Fire and Ash.

"A rock star," Nick said. "I dunno how I can compete with that."

"I'm not sure he identifies as a rock star," Caitlyn said. "Ben's very down-to-earth."

"So, what went wrong?" Nick asked.

Caitlyn shrugged. "Nothing really. We just went on a few dates, but we were always so busy, and if he wasn't tired, then I was. Things just sort of fizzled. I guess that's why a lot of celebrity relationships don't make it...I mean, I'm hardly a celebrity."

"But you should be," Nick said. "I thought for sure you would replace Anne-Marie."

"Maya made a better Lucy than I would have," Caitlyn said. "I'm fine with the way things turned out. If my time with Tiffany has taught me anything, it's that I like performing for an audience when I'm on stage, but I don't want to keep up the performance after the show is over, you know? Plus, there's some really weird people out there, even before you factor in faeries and elementalists."

"I'm glad you don't count me as weird people," Nick said.

"Who says I don't?" Caitlyn grinned and nudged him in the arm with her shoulder. "I do have to be up early to help with auditions tomorrow," she said. "We should head back." To her surprise, Nick put his arm around her as they reversed course.

"What do you think is going on now?" Nick indicated a crowd of reporters in front of Avalon when they reached the entrance.

Caitlyn pulled out her phone. "I don't see any news alerts. Probably just bugging Tiffany or Morgan for updates on Amber. I doubt the hospital will talk to them. Come on. There's a way to access the stairs around the back, if you don't mind a little exercise." She reached for his hand.

Nick looked nervous. "Isn't that where Amber was attacked?"

"I'm sure there's extra security now." Caitlyn tried to sound confident, but a shiver ran up her spine. She began to regret her shortcut when she heard a thump and a low growl near a dumpster in the back alley. Caitlyn thought she caught a glimpse of something black and furry with a tail. Soul Eater?

Nick's grip tightened on her hand.

chapter thirty

"Is someone there?" Caitlyn called.

"Are you crazy?" Nick hissed under his breath. "Nothing good can come from talking to strange people in dark alleys. That's, like, Survival 101."

"It's okay," a familiar voice called back. "It's only me."

Randy rose up behind the dumpster, only his head, chest, and shoulders visible—his *bare* chest and shoulders, Caitlyn realized. A hysterical giggle bubbled up in her throat. She forced it back down to ask, "What are you doing back there?"

"Investigating," Randy said. "I, uh, thought I saw an intruder hide behind the dumpster before you two showed up. You really shouldn't be back here. It's not safe. If you don't mind, I'll just be on my way back inside." He stepped out from behind the dumpster, carrying a couple broken-down boxes to hide his front and back side as he walked past Caitlyn and Nick to access the door to the stairwell.

"Well, that's something you don't see every day," Nick said after Randy was gone. He turned to Caitlyn, looking flummoxed. "Friend of yours? You don't seem all that surprised."

"Oh, I've seen Randy naked before," Caitlyn tried to reassure Nick.

"You don't have to explain yourself to me," Nick said. "I'm in no position to judge."

Caitlyn's eyes widened. "It's not like that," she said. "He can turn into a wolf."

Nick's brow furrowed. "Now I might be judging a little."

Caitlyn refrained from rolling her eyes. Instead, she gave him a patient smile. "He used to be Tiffany's personal bodyguard in Los Angeles, but they're dating now so it's inappropriate," she said. "Now he just helps with hotel security."

"The world's biggest pop star is dating a werewolf." Nick looked dazed. "Wow…"

Caitlyn linked her arm with his as they walked to the door. She didn't bother correcting Nick on the distinction between werewolves and shapeshifters who turned into wolves. There were some things he just wasn't ready to know about yet.

"So," Caitlyn said as she stopped in front of the door to her suite and turned to look at Nick. "This is me."

"No," Nick said patiently, "it's a door."

Caitlyn raised an eyebrow.

"It's a joke, Scully." Nick grinned.

"And we're back on the detective names," Caitlyn said, smiling back at him. "You know, friends call me Cat."

"Is that what we are?" Nick asked. "Friends?"

Caitlyn didn't answer. Instead, she leaned forward to kiss his cheek, but Nick pulled her in for a real kiss that left her breathless and reeling. "Good night, Nick," she said, sporting what she knew had to be a ridiculous smile once she regained her bearings.

"Good night," he said as Caitlyn opened the door to her suite and stepped inside. "Cat."

After Nick turned to walk away, Caitlyn shut the door and leaned back against it.

"Shower, then bed," she told herself. "*Cold* shower."

Okay, maybe lukewarm, Caitlyn decided as she checked the water and recoiled..

Until the chance encounter with Randy, Caitlyn was beginning to feel like a regular girl on a date with her regular…um, boyfriend? Was that how she should think of Nick, or was she jumping the gun? He did seem to be asking if they were more than just friends. Friends generally didn't kiss, after all, Caitlyn decided as she dried off after her shower.

At least not that long or that deeply…

Caitlyn grimaced at her flushed face in the mirror, dressing for bed.

Should she even be pursuing a relationship while her friend was in the hospital and a killer was still on the loose? Never mind Tiffany's residency. Maybe Caitlyn shouldn't have any distractions right now. She tried to push thoughts of Nick and the Vegas Ripper out of her mind. When that failed, Caitlyn turned on the TV.

A documentary on the original Jack the Ripper caught her attention. Obviously, a cynical bid to exploit renewed interest, but Caitlyn found herself unable to disengage.

chapter thirty-one

C aitlyn awoke with an unhappy groan when her alarm went off the next morning, interrupting a dream just as it was getting interesting. She considered hitting snooze, but the alarm was already set for her drop-dead time to get ready for auditions. At least that creepy documentary hadn't given her nightmares.

Caitlyn dressed in a pink tank top and black leggings and pulled her hair back into a loose ponytail. She caught up with Emi and Jade at the elevator.

"Who's the guy?" Jade asked.

"You saw us?"

"We just got back from a late dinner," Emi said. "I'm not surprised you didn't notice us. You seemed pretty...distracted." She grinned.

"I promise I won't let it interfere with my performance," Caitlyn blurted out.

"Omigod, Cat. Relax," Emi said, giggling. "Jade has someone, and I decided to take Charlie up on his offer. He's taking me out Friday night." The elevator arrived. She walked in. Jade and Caitlyn followed.

"Sorry," Caitlyn said when the door closed behind them. "It just feels sort of...wrong, you know? All things considered."

"Amber of all people will not begrudge you romance," Emi said.

Caitlyn knew she was right.

"You still haven't told us anything about him," Jade said.

The elevator stopped.

"He's...Nick," Caitlyn said, not knowing where to begin as they walked to a side door of the theater. "He was the fiancé in *Dracula*, but Broadway didn't work out for him either, so he moved here to earn enough money from bartending to move to California and try his luck at Holly-wood instead."

"Ugh," said Jade. "An actor?"

"So, what happens if he moves away and you're still here doing the show?" Emi asked.

"I hadn't thought that far ahead," Caitlyn answered, her frown deepening.

"Wow," Jade said, as they entered the theater. "Good turnout."

Caitlyn was surprised to see how many men and women had shown up to audition. Not quite as many as the first time, but that was before a performer almost died. Caitlyn's eyes widened when she recognized one of the women auditioning for the show.

What was her name again?

Selina, Caitlyn remembered. The aerial gymnast on Fremont Street who tore into Caitlyn for investigating the murders. Selina met her eyes and smiled. It was not a friendly smile. Caitlyn could only hope she didn't sing and dance as well as she soared through the air.

As it turned out, Selina had no intention of auditioning for Amber's role. Instead, she easily snagged one of the two aerial gymnast openings. Her command of the silks was incredible. Caitlyn wasn't about to speak against her. The other opening went to a man named Obi who used to perform with Cirque du Soleil. He had even competed in other forms of gymnastics on the Olympic team for Nigeria. Just an all-around gifted athlete and performer.

Tiffany thanked anyone who only came to audition for those openings. "We'll continue with dancing and singing tomorrow," she told the rest.

Jade walked across the stage to congratulate Selina and Obi. She began to have an animated conversation in Spanish with Selina, glancing back at

Caitlyn a couple of times. Caitlyn's Spanish was a little rusty, but she recognized a few words like gato and estúpida.

"Do you know her?" Emi asked.

"Sort of," Caitlyn said. "It's a long story."

"Well, if it isn't the dancing detective," Selina said, walking over with Jade.

"This little weirdo tried to go undercover and interrogate people who knew the Ripper's victims a few weeks ago," Jade told Emi. She turned to Caitlyn and grasped her shoulder. "You're amazing," she said.

Selina laughed, looking more amused than angry.

Emi gave Caitlyn an incredulous look.

"That pretty much sums it up," Caitlyn said, grimacing. "Congratulations," she told Selina. "You were amazing."

"Angel tried to talk me into the first round of auditions, but she wouldn't have been able to make it work with her school schedule, and I wasn't about to audition without her. Guess she gave me an extra push from beyond," Selina said.

Still feeling mortified, Caitlyn passed on joining them for lunch, even though Selina didn't seem to hold a grudge after all. Instead, she visited Jax and Zaya.

Nick had picked up an extra shift at work, but he messaged Caitlyn in the afternoon to say how much he enjoyed their date. She happily sailed through the rest of the day.

The audition turnout was much smaller on Tuesday without any men and a lot less women, only a dozen after the original thirty or so. Tiffany started by having the auditioners sing solos. Emi knew how to play piano, so she accompanied them, leaving Tiffany, Caitlyn, and Jade to judge their performances. They narrowed their choice down to three women.

Tiffany's choreographer, Natasha, was back in town to help teach Amber's replacement. After the remaining women took a break for a light lunch, she taught them one of the more challenging routines while Tiffany, Caitlyn, Jade, and Emi went down to the hotel buffet, where they found Zaya stuffing her face full of fruit and dessert while Jax looked on.

"She never ate like this back home," Jax said.

"Food never tasted like this back home," Zaya said around a mouthful of chocolate cake.

"We start rehearsing again on Thursday," Tiffany told Jax as she sat down with a plate full of fruit and sushi. "Any plans for keeping Zaya entertained?"

"Morgan hired a tutor," Jax said with a sidelong glance at Caitlyn.

"I'm surprised she found the time now that she has that creepy kidnapper and his lawyer girlfriend to deal with," Jade said. "Emi and I saw them on the news last night. Apparently, his whole campaign will revolve around bringing the so-called Fae menace to justice."

"What's he running for, anyway?" Caitlyn asked.

"The Senate," Emi said, "but for the whole country, not just New York. He's scary."

"No," Jade said. "The House. He wouldn't stand a chance, otherwise."

"I can't imagine a monster like that winning no matter what he ran for, and where," Tiffany said, "but stranger things have happened."

Jax looked bewildered and Zaya just looked bored.

"They're talking about this really bad guy who used to be imprisoned but now he's free for some dumb reason, and he's trying to get more power," Caitlyn explained. She didn't want to go into too much detail since Jade and Emi's knowledge was limited so she decided to give them the broad strokes. "He also has a grudge against Mor-"

"Sorry to interrupt," Tiffany said, "but the topic of Emerson Fowler turns my stomach."

"Between that crazy guy and the Ripper still on the loose," Caitlyn said, "it's always something, isn't it? Oh, did I tell you? There was a documentary on the other night, and they talked all about how Jack the Ripper—"

"That's an even worse topic," Tiffany interrupted with a pointed glance at Zaya.

"Sorry." Caitlyn busied herself eating fries and sushi.

The audition resumed after lunch. First the three women performed the dance routine for "Under Your Spell" together. Then they took turns dancing with Caitlyn, Jade, and Emi. "I'm sorry," Tiffany said after they all performed. "I'd like to hear how well you harmonize before I make a decision. I know you've been dancing for a few hours, but it's good to see how well your voice can hold up to singing and dancing."

After the women were done, Tiffany deliberated with Caitlyn, Jade, and Emi backstage.

"Grace has a great voice, but she was shaky on the lyra and stumbled through the dance routine," Emi said.

"Melody was fine on the lyra, and great at dancing, but she got breathless halfway through when we added vocals," Jade said.

"And Skylar was good at everything, but not great," Caitlyn said. "Now what?"

"If Melody struggled with one song, that doesn't bode well for a whole show, and we don't really have time to work out the kinks with Grace, so Skylar seems like the best choice," Tiffany said. "Guess I'll go out and break the news."

"Do we have to come with?" Emi asked. "Because I'd like to be elsewhere."

"Same," Caitlyn agreed.

"I'll do it," Jade said, shrugging. "We've all been on the other side of things. I dunno about you two, but I appreciate someone that has enough respect to look me in the eyes and break the news gently."

"Gently" wasn't a word Caitlyn associated with Jade. Tiffany talked instead with Jade standing on one side, and Caitlyn and Emi on the other, sufficiently shamed by Jade. Grace and Melody looked disappointed but hugged Skylar, who beamed with excitement.

"You have tomorrow off," Tiffany said, "but then we're back to work bright and early Thursday morning to get the show back on track."

"I won't let you down," Skylar said. "I can't wait to work with everyone," she told Caitlyn, Jade, and Emi, but she looked nervous.

Caitlyn considered how daunting joining a group that had performed together for a couple years must be. "You should join us for dinner tomorrow." She spit the invitation out faster than Jade could kick her shin. "What?" she said after Skylar left. "We should help her feel welcome. How else will she go from good to great?"

"I know," Jade said. "I was just hoping to enjoy one last night of freedom."

"We still have weekends off," Emi reminded her.

Caitlyn, too, had been spoiled by the time off. She wondered if things with Nick would fizzle the way they did with Ben, especially once the show premiered. Or maybe the Ripper would return and render all of her relationship fears moot. She shivered.

chapter thirty-two

Tiffany released a statement Wednesday morning announcing the new performers joining the show and reiterating her love and support of Amber. Though she no longer employed a personal assistant, Tiffany didn't stick around to see the response. She just made her posts as needed and moved on with her life. It was the only way to maintain her sanity.

Tiffany had a harder time evading unwanted press courtesy of Emerson Fowler and "Veronica Highmore." A reporter disguised as a tourist in a loose shirt and cargo shorts had accosted her in line at the Bluebelle Bakery this morning to ask about allegations of staging Amber's assault. *To what end*, Tiffany refrained from asking aloud. Instead, she waited for hotel security to remove the pushy reporter.

"Amber almost died," she said as they led him away. "Show some respect."

Someone patted her shoulder, but most people looked away to hide that they had been watching, or they continued talking to each other in furtive whispers. When she returned to her suite, Tiffany found contact information for D'Andre Jones on her phone. Instead of emailing, she tried calling. He picked up right away.

"Tiffany Sharp," D'Andre answered in his silky-smooth voice, "to what do I owe the pleasure?"

"I know this isn't the usual way of doing things," Tiffany said, "but I was wondering if you had an opening in your schedule for me to fly you out to Las Vegas to do a segment on my upcoming residency at the Avalon Hotel and Casino. I'd love to share a sneak peek of the show with your viewers."

"I didn't get to where I am today by going about things the usual way," D'Andre said. Tiffany remembered the role he played in her escape from Brendan. His connection to the Fae had led to his job on *Entertainment Daily* after they fired the woman who outed Tiffany's questionable origin. "And the network did want me to see about sending out a reporter," D'Andre continued, "but I'd be more than happy to make the trip myself."

"Wonderful," Tiffany said. "Rehearsals start back up tomorrow, but the week after next would be great if there's a date and time that works for you."

A feeling of relief came over Tiffany as she ironed out the details with D'Andre. She didn't worry about bad publicity hurting the show. The first month and a half were on track to selling out, in fact. But Tiffany did want to make sure at least some people were coming for the actual show and not the just drama behind the scenes. After all, the busiest day of sales so far had immediately followed the Ripper's attack on Amber.

"We're beginning to think Convict Two skipped town after all," Randy said the next morning while Tiffany got ready for rehearsal. "Anna doesn't want to reduce hotel security, but I think my nightly sweeps are coming to an end." He sat on the bed to take off his shoes.

"That's wonderful," Tiffany said as she pulled a tank top over her sports bra. "It's a shame 'Veronica Highmore' is using his absence after Amber's attack as proof Morgan was involved. Me, too. I know I shouldn't look myself up online, but I don't want to bury my head in the sand either. The things people are saying…" Tiffany shuddered. "I wonder if Vivienne knows her sister is missing."

"I wonder if she knows *why* Morgan is missing," Randy said, his tone darkening.

Tiffany's eyes widened. "Do you think she has something to do with it?"

"Not sure," Randy said, "but Lance and I have discussed the possibility. As far as any of Morgan's people know, Vivienne's been cooped up in her tower in the otherworld this whole time. They're all as blindsided by her return to this world as you are. Even if she isn't involved, she's bound to notice something off. We're trying to limit Anna's public appearances, but she has an interview with the paper tomorrow morning."

"I'm flying out D'Andre Jones from *Entertainment Daily* next week," Tiffany said.

"You don't think he's going to pull the rug out from under you like the last time you appeared on *Entertainment Daily*, do you?" Randy looked concerned.

"No, even if I didn't trust D'Andre, he wouldn't risk losing his ties to the Fae. It's part of why the network hired him in place of their old host." Tiffany tried and failed to hide her smile.

"You're so cute when you're being petty." Randy rose from the bed to kiss Tiffany's cheek. He wrapped his arms around her waist and nuzzled her neck. "When does rehearsal start?"

"In less than ten minutes," Tiffany said, glancing at the alarm clock.

"That's not nearly enough time for what I had in mind." Randy reluctantly let go.

"We'll catch up soon." Tiffany pulled him back for a quick kiss that lingered so long she barely arrived in time for rehearsal.

"Wow," Caitlyn said. "You're all flushed, and we haven't even started yet."

"Busy morning," Tiffany said, still trying to catch her breath as she joined them on stage.

"I'll bet it was." Jade exchanged a grin with Emi.

Skylar looked confused. She had blond hair like Amber, only lighter and shoulder-length, presently pulled back into a couple braided pigtails, and blue eyes instead of brown.

"Tiffany's boyfriend is really hot," Emi explained. "In a scruffy wolfish kind of way."

"Okay," Tiffany interrupted, trying not to telegraph how on-the-nose Emi's description really was. Only Caitlyn knew the truth, and she preferred to keep it that way. "We just have a couple of days to catch Skylar up on choreography before the rest of the performers come back next week, so we should get focused."

Fortunately, Skylar was a quick study. "I've watched your concert so many times," she said. "My roommates and I practiced all the routines. I'm really glad you kept a lot of the same choreography. But it still feels fresh," Skylar was quick to amend.

"Relax," Jade said. "Tiffany doesn't bite."

"Does Randy?" Emi asked.

"Of course," Caitlyn said, "He's *Randy*."

Emi giggled. Even Skylar laughed.

"Stop that!" Tiffany took off the scrunchie that secured her ponytail and threw it at Caitlyn.

In truth, Tiffany was grateful for the sense of normalcy as they danced and laughed. With a pang, she thought of Amber and how much she missed her. She could tell the others felt the loss, but they didn't let that stop them from welcoming Skylar into the fold. She had big shoes to fill, and not just because Amber wore a size ten.

"I just wanted to thank you again for this opportunity," Skylar said after rehearsal when the others had gone. "My parents tried to talk me out of auditioning, but they worry too much. I can't wait to tell them you're like a real girl in person. I don't care what they say on TV."

Tiffany forced a smile. "Thanks," she said.

"Regular girl, I mean." Skylar frowned. "Obviously, you're real. I mean, there you are. I've never worked with a star before. Let alone someone who's literally out of this world." She gave a nervous smile.

"It's fine," Tiffany said, and she meant it. She was used to people stumbling over their words when they first had a chance to talk to her, even before the truth came out. And now that people knew she was part-Fae, it helped having a barometer of what they thought. So why did Skylar's words feel like such a punch to the gut?

chapter thirty-three

Tiffany still didn't get to spend a lot of time with Randy until the weekend, when he had readjusted to her schedule. She sometimes wondered if working nights was his natural state, but Randy assured her shapeshifters could be adaptable. He didn't like to talk about his old life before his homeworld exiled him, so she had learned not to ask too many questions. Randy, or rather, Randolph, wasn't even his real name, though he might have picked something different had he known how much amusement his nickname provided her friends.

Caitlyn tried to talk her into a double date Sunday night, but Tiffany wanted to keep Randy all to herself. She wasn't happy to find out Nick knew Randy was a shapeshifter, either, even though she understood why Caitlyn had to provide an explanation.

"Why didn't you tell me about Caitlyn and her friend running into you in the alley?" Tiffany asked Randy over dinner.

"Honestly," Randy said, looking down as he cut his steak into smaller pieces, "I'd forgotten all about it by the time I saw you the next morning. I wish Caitlyn hadn't told him so much, but I guess it would be hard to explain away the nudity otherwise." He looked up with a rueful grin. "I suppose I could have stayed in wolf form, but even if Caitlyn recognized me, I had no idea how he'd react. What if he had a weapon?"

"Fair point," Tiffany said. She winced at the thought of someone hurting Randy. He'd survived flames and electrocution, but how would he fare against a bullet? Or would it have to be silver to hurt him?

That's werewolves, Tiffany reminded herself. *Make-believe.*

"So, when does D'Andre get here?" Randy asked.

"Wednesday."

"Anything I can do to help?"

"Just refrain from any streaking," Tiffany teased.

"So, I can't give them the full Monty?" Randy feigned a pout.

"Definitely not," Tiffany said. "It's a family show."

Tiffany visited Amber with Caitlyn after rehearsal on Monday. They were surprised to see her out of bed in a sweatshirt and leggings, a smaller bandage on her neck. She looked a lot less pale and her hair was neatly braided. Amber still had her whiteboard close at hand. She picked it up, pressing her lips together as she wrote and erased a few times before holding the board up for them to read her message.

Looks like I'm on the home stretch.

"That's awesome!" Caitlyn shouted, then slapped a hand over her mouth.

Amber wrote something else: *they expect to discharge me some time this week. My parents are already making outpatient arrangements for me back home.*

"That's great news," Tiffany said. She tried to smile, but her eyes must have given her away because Amber set down the board and gestured for a hug from both Tiffany and Caitlyn. Somehow, they made the awkward group hug work, crying and laughing. Well, Tiffany and Caitlyn cried and laughed. Amber just wiped away a small tear when they separated.

So, how's the new girl? Amber wrote.

"She's no *you*," Tiffany said. "But she's a fast learner."

Is she pretty?

"Eh," Caitlyn said. "She's alright, I guess."

Liar, Amber wrote. Her grin widened as she wrote something else. *Miguel visited a couple more times. Brought me chocolate as soon as he knew I was eating solids.* Amber indicated an elegant gold and cream box on the counter. *Try a piece.*

Caitlyn selected a piece and took a bite with a rapturous expression.

"Keep him," she said, eyes wide. "No, wait—see if he'll smuggle in some wine to go with that chocolate, then keep him." She held the box out to Tiffany.

"Have mine," Tiffany said.

"You're the best," Caitlyn squealed. Then she turned to Amber. "No, *you're* the best."

Miguel is the best, Amber wrote, laughing. *You can't have Miguel*. She gave Caitlyn a stern look.

"I think Caitlyn already has someone," Tiffany said, chuckling.

Caitlyn spent the rest of the visit catching Amber up. And Tiffany for that matter. She didn't know that much about Nick herself, though something about Caitlyn's cagey looks made Tiffany think she was leaving out some important details.

Or maybe Tiffany was reading too much into things because she still had trust issues after Brendan. Had she not grilled Randy the day before?

Sienna surprised Tiffany with a hug as they were leaving. "Your last album has grown on me," she said. "You should do acoustic music more often. Or maybe a rock album!"

"I'll think about it." Tiffany smiled.

Tiffany debated whether she should introduce the world to Perry the python when D'Andre arrived on Wednesday or save him for the live show. After her backup singers assured Tiffany that the biggest draw was herself and not an homage to one of her idols, she decided to let the television crew film "Free 2 Dance" for her segment.

D'Andre brought only a camera woman and a sound guy with him. The camera woman was an enthusiastic college student named Ling who couldn't stop gushing over the stage design and costumes. "It's her first gig on location," D'Andre told Tiffany, "But she's a total pro. Came to the studio as an intern and turned it into a full-time gig. She's got her sights on directing."

"Maybe we should get her in touch with Gabrielle," Tiffany said.

"Already thought about it," D'Andre said, "but she's currently filming on location somewhere in eastern Europe. A remote village. Sent me some blurry video of these creepy little rodents that keep chewing on her equipment—and her crew," he added under his breath. "Very not of this earth, if you know what I mean."

Tiffany had a bad feeling she knew exactly what he meant.

D'andre accepted a microphone from the outstretched hand of the sound guy, Steve. "I'll stick to the questions I sent in advance," he said. "No surprises."

Ling rejoined them on stage with her camera and a ring light. Tiffany coordinated with the makeup artist for her show to do a trial run today before tech rehearsals started next week. Chantel touched up Tiffany's makeup while Steve performed a sound check.

After the interview, Tiffany changed out of her tank top and tights into her costume for the second act of the show. She wore a gold bikini top and a skirt made of different colored strands of filmy chiffon that revealed a gold bikini bottom when she spun around. Chantel upped the drama from the more natural makeup look Tiffany sported during her interview. Then she applied body glitter to all visible skin, which was a lot.

"It's a whole new world," Miguel quipped as he and Justin took turns handling Perry in their own skin-baring costumes for the first time. They wore only tight faux leather pants and matching black boots with suede soles. No body glitter, but either lotion or nervous sweat added a glossy sheen to their muscles as the python wrapped itself around their shoulders and biceps.

"So magical," Justin agreed, tightening his jaw.

Perry remained quiet, thankfully. That is, until it came time to perform.

"Sssomething is ssstirring," he hissed in Tiffany's ear after Miguel and Justin draped him over her shoulders. She almost screamed but kept her cool for the camera. Tiffany had long since ruled out psychosis for herself, but she was starting to wonder if reptiles could have mental health problems, too. She knew cats and dogs did, and maybe birds did, too—so why not snakes?

"The Ripper?"

"Sssomething older..."

Tiffany felt a twinge of guilt contemplating if life in captivity had damaged Perry's psyche. Sure, the hotel was built on top of a mysterious vortex, but nothing in any known universe could break through ten feet of cement.

"Ignore me at your own peril," Perry continued.

Crazy and pretentious, Tiffany thought, *what a combo.* Unless Perry had any new information about Convict Two, he could tell his story walking— or rather, slithering. She masked her agitation behind a sultry smile as she worked the stage.

The performance otherwise went well. Tiffany didn't think anyone noticed her exchange with Perry until Caitlyn, wearing a metallic purple bikini with hot pants, caught up with her backstage. "The snake said something again, didn't he?" she whispered. "Is the Ripper back?"

Tiffany shook her head. "We'll talk later."

chapter thirty-four

"The snake thinks something is under the hotel," Tiffany told Caitlyn when she joined the pop star and Randy for dinner in their hotel suite after rehearsal.

Caitlyn cringed, picking at her dinner roll. "That's not creepy at all."

"Technically, Las Vegas sits on a series of fault lines," Randy said, "but most earthquakes here are too small to feel. It's possible he's more attuned, being a snake and all." Caitlyn didn't miss the look that passed between him and Tiffany.

"If we were on the ground floor, maybe, but the theater is on the second," she said.

"Pythons are arboreal," Randy said. "They live in trees."

"I know what arboreal means," Caitlyn said, scowling. Her expression softened after she buttered her roll and took a bite. *Yummy.* She finished it and reached for another while they were still warm.

"You never told me how your latest date with Nick went," Tiffany said, sounding anxious to change the subject away from earthquakes and scaly portents of doom.

Caitlyn sighed. "Great," she said. "Don't tell 'Morgan' on me, but we went to you-know-where for their Tournament of Kings. Seemed a little early in the relationship to share a meal you have to tear apart with your fingers, but it was fun."

"So why do you look so unhappy?" Tiffany asked. "No butterflies?"

"Butterflies?" Caitlyn repeated. "More like bats."

Deja vu.

"What do bats have to do with jousting?" Randy appeared confused.

"Nothing," Tiffany said, laughing. "It's a metaphor. It means Caitlyn's into him. A lot. Caitlyn?"

"What?" Caitlyn shook herself. "Sorry. Talking about bats made me remember *Dracula*. Not so much the Nick stuff," she said with a sidelong glance at Randy, who didn't need all the details of her boyfriend's questionable past, "but the other stuff that happened."

"You're worried about opening night in a few weeks, aren't you?" Tiffany reached across the dining table to pat Caitlyn's hand. "We did a whole world tour together, and nothing happened," she said. "You're not cursed. And Nick isn't even in the show, but maybe you should invite him to a different night if you're worried about it."

"I'm being ridiculous, I know," Caitlyn said.

"No, you've been through a lot the past few years. And after the Vegas Ripper, everyone's nerves are shot," Tiffany said.

"Do we really think he's gone?" Caitlyn asked.

"Ninety-nine-point-nine percent positive," Randy said.

"That point-zero-one gives you just enough leeway to cover your ass," Caitlyn said, but she smiled at Randy. He gave her a good-natured shrug in return.

Tiffany ran everyone through the full show on Thursday. No makeup and costumes this time, but Caitlyn was pleased to see how quickly Skylar caught on. She even looked better on the lyra, but unlike Caitlyn, she had prior experience. So, that was okay—but Caitlyn considered coming in early on Friday to iron out a few kinks. Skylar sounded better, too. She was no Amber, but she harmonized well.

Everyone but Skylar had just enough time to get to the hospital with Tiffany to say goodbye to Amber. She was being discharged and would be flying home with her family that night on a redeye. After everyone was done saying their goodbyes, including Miguel, who also put in appearance, she looked like she'd already flown on a redeye. They all did.

Stay out of trouble, she wrote to Caitlyn specifically.

"I *am* the trouble," Caitlyn said. That got a laugh from everyone.

Good. Caitlyn didn't like things to be so serious for so long. She gave Amber one last hug and linked arms with Jade and Emi. Emi leaned her head against Caitlyn's shoulder.

Miguel was helping the Mills carry out stuffed animals and other gifts, so the only thing left to do was watch as Amber walked out with Miguel and her family. She turned and waved one last time.

"Do you think they'll require the bear to have its own ticket?" Caitlyn asked.

"Cat." Emi and Jade groaned. Tiffany just smiled and shook her head.

Caitlyn awoke to a text from Nick on Friday morning.

Didn't Entertainment Daily *just film you guys? They're already airing promos. I saw you a couple times on the hoop. You looked good.*

Caitlyn flushed with pleasure. Then she chided herself. Like he would tell her if she looked awful. He was just being polite. She refrained from asking for more details and typed a simple *Thanks* with a kissy face. Then she deleted the kissy face and went with a wink instead.

Her phone chirped again while she was getting ready.

Can't wait to see you in person again.

And just like that Caitlyn knew she would be thinking of nothing else the rest of the day. Good thing she could basically sleepwalk through the show at this point, but she should probably focus when she was on the lyra now that the crew was raising it for parts of some numbers.

Caitlyn took Jax and Zaya to dinner and a movie after rehearsal. Despite being the youngest performer, Jax held his own. The other fire dancers didn't understand why he prepped alone, but they accepted that he had his own methods Tiffany was incorporating into the show. Caitlyn merely shrugged and smiled when people expressed wonder at his abilities. So far, the existence of elementalists was not as well-known as the Fae were, but she heard a few whispers.

Jax and Zaya had never seen a movie before. They were enthralled by the images on the screen. Imagine impressing kids who could shoot fireballs from the palms of their hands. Caitlyn had chosen a reasonably family-friendly superhero film that didn't require a lot of homework—or brain power—from what the reviews indicated.

"We should make costumes," Zaya told her brother as they ate ice cream sundaes after the movie. "Then we can fight crime. The Ripper would never come back to town if he knew we were around to light him up."

"Easy, Zaya," Jax said. "Setting people on fire is frowned upon here, just like home."

"Even bad guys?" Zaya pouted.

"Even bad guys," Caitlyn said. "We can defend ourselves if someone tries to hurt us, but we can't use excessive force." That just led to a big discussion on law and ethics that was above Caitlyn's pay grade, but fortunately their own world had enough structure that Jax appeared to be able to reason with his sister.

Zaya still seemed pretty hyped about getting a costume and a mask.

Caitlyn didn't blame her.

Saturday felt like a slog despite time at the pool with Jax and Zaya and dinner and dancing with Emi and Jade, both of whom had dates, leaving Caitlyn as the fifth wheel.

But Sunday.

Sunday meant seeing Nick again. But what if Nick changed his mind? What if he decided he was bored of her? Or what if Caitlyn decided she was bored of Nick? What if Perry the Python was right, and the big one was coming, and the earth was going to split open and swallow Avalon whole before she even had a chance at another kiss?

Caitlyn had experienced several earthquakes living in Los Angeles. She slept through some small ones, endured more moderate ones while she was awake, and once an earthquake strong enough to bounce her out of bed scared the metaphorical crap out of her. She had not appreciated that rude awakening. Not at all.

And now Caitlyn sat alone in her suite, the saddest girl to ever indulge in a delicious maple- frosted cream-filled donut covered in bits of bacon, until Nick messaged her to confirm their date that evening.

I'd love to spend the day with you, but yesterday was rough. Had to break up a nasty fight and stay after my shift talking to cops. Gonna try to get a little more sleep and take it easy so you don't have to deal with me being grumpy.

Caitlyn shivered. She had been so busy worrying about big ones and serial killers that she forgot all about the more mundane threats that accompanied daily life. *I'm glad you're okay,* she typed back. *Can't wait to see you.*

"Most people say 'hi' first," Nick said after a long lingering kiss.

"Sorry."

"Not complaining." Nick grinned. "Now remind me why I'm wearing this suit. I feel a little overdressed just to visit you at your hotel." He leaned in for another kiss, bracing an arm against the doorway.

Caitlyn ducked under his arm and stepped into the hall. "Dan gave you his Cirque du Soleil tickets because he broke up with the Sharpie and didn't want them to go to waste," she said. "Plus, I got all pretty." She gestured at the strapless black velvet evening dress Tiffany had loaned her, one of the benefits of sharing a dress size with a wealthy pop star. Emi had helped her style her long brown hair in gentle curls down her back.

"You were already pretty," Nick said. "Fine. Dinner and a show it is," he said with mock disappointment. "I hope you brought your appetite."

She snickered. "Have you met me?"

Caitlyn felt like a pop star herself when Nick opened the door to his Corvette. Not that she cared about fancy cars, but they looked ridiculously picture-perfect in their evening wear as they headed out for a night on the town. Part of her wish they'd stayed in, but she was trying to behave. And who could pass up Cirque du Soleil and five-star dining?

"Oh wow," Caitlyn breathed as she walked with Nick under a canopy of white and purple flowers when they arrived at the restaurant. "This place is amazing."

"Yeah, I think Dan was going to propose tonight," Nick said. "Can't believe she dumped him when she found out he planned to open a practice in a rural town after he graduates. He can do better. Really hard to get a reservation here, too."

Not the cheapest place, either. Caitlyn had sticker shock when she looked at the menu after they sat in an intimate booth with tan leather seats and a dark wooden table. Avalon had some fancier restaurants to choose from, but even Tiffany usually stuck with the less expensive steak-house. The other one was as famous for its small portions as its flavors.

"Should we order a bottle of wine?" Nick asked.

"Too many choices," Caitlyn said. "Ooh, it's social hour. Is that like happy hour? We can do cocktails and share dim sum. Everything looks so good. We have to get the calamari, and the sesame shrimp, and whatever those fancy bird-looking things are."

"Yeah, I saw the dinner prices, too," Nick said. "But dim sum does sound good."

"Good thing I only need chopsticks here," Caitlyn said after the server brought place settings and martinis with beautiful orchids the server assured her were edible. "I'd be hosed if I had to tell a salad fork apart from a dinner fork like the fancy places in Avalon."

"I always thought the little forks and spoons were for kids, and the big forks and spoons were for adults," Nick teased. "And my family owns a restaurant chain."

After their amazing dinner, Caitlyn was even more dazzled by the show. Not only did it include aerial gymnastics that made her relieved she'd never have to ascend anywhere near as high for Tiffany's show, but there were even swordfights and martial arts.

"I thought you might like the swordplay after *Dracula*," Nick said as Caitlyn kept raving on their way up the elevator at Avalon. "I heard a rumor you took out one of those hellhounds with a prop sword. Mean-while, I got slashed to ribbons trying to help people backstage and ended up getting a rabies series. Do those things even get Earth diseases, or should I be worried about some sort of wacky space rabies instead?"

"If you haven't gone rabid yet," Caitlyn said as they exited the elevator and walked to her suite, "I think you're okay."

"I dunno," Nick said. "You're looking awfully bite-able." He leaned down and nibbled on Caitlyn's ear and neck.

She closed her eyes but felt someone staring. When she opened them, she saw a stooped old man with a housekeeping cart watching them. He had glittering malevolent eyes and appeared to wink before continuing down the hall. He walked with a distinct limp.

Caitlyn gasped.

chapter thirty-five

"Perhaps we should move this inside," Nick said, straightening.

Wordlessly, Caitlyn unlocked the door and pulled him inside. "Did you see him?"

"See who?" Nick asked, raising an eyebrow as he removed his jacket and draped it over the back of a dining chair.

"The old man with the cart," Caitlyn said. "He was limping. Did you see him?"

"Maybe he'd rather work than sit at home collecting disability." Nick shrugged. "Some people like to keep working in their old age. I'm sure he's fine." He put his hands in his dress pockets, gazing at Caitlyn with a mild expression.

"That's not what I meant," Caitlyn said. "I probably shouldn't be telling you this, but the Vegas Ripper is one of the Fae. That's why he got away despite security busting his leg open. He's super powerful...but not so powerful the injury wouldn't cause permanent damage."

"I remember seeing the security footage of the attack on the news," Nick said. "That guy was, like, forty, tops."

"Yeah, well, the Vegas Ripper is way older than that. So was Leanne in New York. Remember her?"

Nick nodded, raising an eyebrow.

"The Fae can look however they want," Caitlyn continued. "The original Jack the Ripper was never even caught. Did you know that? They thought they found evidence tying some creepy dude to the murders long after the fact, but there were too many discrepancies. That's because the real Ripper wasn't human. Probably the same monster who terrorized Atlanta in the early nineteen hundreds. Similar M.O."

"And now you think someone who committed not one but two waves of murders on two different continents without being caught is dumb enough to hang out at the scene of the crime?" Nick looked incredulous. "Do you even hear yourself right now? You sound like you should be flailing your arms in front of one of those maps covered with yarn and newspaper clippings."

"Maybe I should follow him," Caitlyn said. "See what he's up to before I bother anyone else. Maybe you're right and he's just an old man wanting to feel useful."

"And maybe I'm wrong and you're repeating past mistakes," Nick said. "I know you've developed a taste for danger, but can't you just pursue a doomed relationship like the rest of us?"

Caitlyn rolled her eyes, but Nick wasn't finished.

"The last time you did something reckless," he said, "he almost killed your friend."

"Low blow." Caitlyn frowned.

"It's a fair hit," Nick retorted, "and you know it."

"I think we just had our first real fight," Caitlyn said, biting her lip on a smile.

"Probably won't be the last, either, but next time it'll hopefully be over something mundane like what movie to see or whether pineapple belongs on pizza." Nick held out his arms. "C'mere."

Caitlyn accepted the offered hug. "If we can't agree pineapple belongs nowhere near my pizza, I don't know if we can make this last," she teased before pulling away. "I should still tell someone what I saw. That way, security can keep an eye on him, and I don't have to blame myself if someone else gets hurt because I *didn't* do something."

When Caitlyn reached for the doorknob, Nick put a hand over hers. "There's a phone right over there," he said, pointing at a side table. "Stay?"

Caitlyn hesitated. "I thought you said I shouldn't do anything reckless."

"It's a calculated risk," Nick agreed. He reached for Caitlyn's other hand to pull her close.

chapter thirty-six

Nick did not know what time it was when he woke up. He reached out to pull Caitlyn closer. "Caitlyn," he whispered. "Cat?" No answer. Nick patted the bed. The spot where she had been laying felt cool to the touch. Nick swore under his breath.

"Someone needs to put a bell on her."

chapter thirty-seven

T iffany had been dozing with her head on Randy's chest when someone knocked on the door. "Why would someone be here at this hour?" she muttered. The knocking continued. Pushing herself up with a groan, Tiffany searched around the bed in the dark for clothing.

Randy sat up. "I'll get it," he said.

"Don't forget pants," Tiffany reminded him as she pulled a sweatshirt over her camisole just in case. Randy waved her off. After he dressed in a shirt and sleep pants, he walked out of the room and to the front door. Tiffany pulled on a pair of shorts before following behind.

"Caitlyn? What are you doing here so late?" Randy asked after he opened the door.

Caitlyn hurried inside the suite, looking disheveled in a sweatshirt that fell off one shoulder and leggings. She wore mismatched shoes, her hair falling down her back in wild tangles. "Did you get my message?" she asked Tiffany.

"What message?" Tiffany asked. She looked at Randy, who walked to the phone in the living room.

"Damn," he said. "Sorry, Caitlyn." He picked up the phone to check missed messages.

"Caitlyn, what's wrong?" Tiffany asked, reaching for her. "Did something happen to you?"

"No," Caitlyn said. "I just saw something weird and thought you guys should know."

Randy hung up the phone and joined them.

"Thanks," he told Caitlyn. "I'm going downstairs right now to talk to security," he told Tiffany. "You should stay here until we make sure it's safe," he said to Caitlyn.

Caitlyn bit her lip. "Nick's sleeping in my room," she said. "He doesn't even know I left."

"Should be safe," Randy said. "He doesn't fit the profile, and Convict Two won't target you if he expects you to have company."

"Convict Two?" Tiffany's grip on Caitlyn's arm tightened. "He's back?"

"No time to explain," Randy said, slipping into loafers. "Caitlyn can fill you in."

Tiffany turned to Caitlyn.

"We should sit down," Caitlyn told her, walking to the sofa. "You're as white as a ghost." Tiffany sat beside her, and waited. "When we got back, I saw this creepy old man with a housekeeping cart," Caitlyn explained. "He winked at me. Then he limped away."

Tiffany shuddered. "I can't believe he came back here. And he's in the building?!"

"I wonder how he got that cart in the first place. What if he already hurt someone? I should have come here as soon as I called and you didn't answer, but Nick didn't want me to leave." The color drained from Caitlyn's face. "Oh, no."

"What?" Tiffany put a hand on Caitlyn's shoulder.

"What if Nick didn't want me to leave because he has something to do with it? When we first started talking, I accused him of being an imposter, which was dumb because Convict Two would have had no idea we knew each other," Caitlyn said, talking faster. "But that doesn't mean he didn't find out later, and they're working together now."

"Okay," Tiffany said. "Let's slow down a minute. After Brendan, I know what it's like to have trust issues, but this sounds a little far-fetched. Are you sure you're not just…" She trailed off as she tried to find the right words.

"Looking for excuses to bail?" Caitlyn finished, raising an eyebrow.

Tiffany heard a click as the front door unlocked.

Was Randy back already?

Tiffany and Caitlyn exchanged a worried look as the door opened.

"Two-for-one special," an old man warbled as he limped into the room and closed the door. Then Convict Two dropped the façade, his features shifting as he stretched to his full height. He didn't bother maintaining a human appearance. Tiffany recoiled at the sight of his translucent hair and skin, dark fathomless eyes, and jagged teeth, so many teeth when he leered at them. He reached into his uniform and pulled out a wickedly sharp dagger.

Caitlyn sprung into motion, jumping in front of Tiffany to block her. She reached into her sleeve and pulled out a mean-looking dagger of her own. Tiffany thought the Fae had taken her weapons. Maybe she bought her own knife, but this dagger looked like it had otherworldly origins with its jewel-encrusted hilt and shimmering blade.

Convict Two was less impressed. He chuckled as he lurched toward Caitlyn, but he was clearly still hurting from his injuries and didn't move fast enough. Caitlyn snarled, then lunged forward and kicked him, targeting the side of his knee with her foot.

"Get back!" Caitlyn shouted at Tiffany.

Tiffany rose from the couch and ran into the kitchen, hoping to find a weapon of her own. She couldn't let Caitlyn face Convict Two alone. Tiffany didn't make it two steps before someone pushed the front door of the apartment open. Convict Two must not have closed it all the way. Now someone with dark hair walked in. His eyes grew wide as he surveyed the room.

"Nick!" Caitlyn yelled. "No!"

chapter thirty-eight

Caitlyn was feeling pretty good about their chances before Nick showed up. After the soul eaters in New York and the reaver in Los Angeles, she felt like she'd been working her way up to take on the big baddie looming in front of her. Sure, there had been that tiny hiccup with the elementalists and Brendan's mind control, but the Ripper was relying on pure brute force, leaving her mind free to focus on the task at hand. Protect Tiffany and beat the bad guy.

Or at least hold him off until help arrived.

Nick's arrival complicated matters. For a moment, Caitlyn froze, wondering if he had come to help Convict Two finish them off. Time started moving again as Convict Two sneered at Nick over his shoulder before charging at her once more.

Then Nick charged at him. She stepped out of the way as they fell onto the coffee table, then toppled to the floor in a heap. Someone howled in pain. Caitlyn watched in horror as Convict Two, who had ended up on top, raised the knife, now dripping in blood, to stab Nick again.

Caitlyn jumped to close the distance and landed on the coffee table before kicking at Convict Two's wrist. What happened to Amber had been bad enough. She wasn't going to let Convict Two kill Nick after she had the audacity to doubt him. The knife flew out of his hand. Caitlyn dropped her own knife and ran for his. Convict Two turned to grab at her ankle, rolling off of Nick, who groaned in pain.

Caitlyn wrenched her ankle free and grabbed the knife. She turned to face Convict Two, crouching low. Nick released another low groan. A growing dark stain spread across the waistline of his formerly white dress shirt. Caitlyn felt torn between running to his aid or focusing on Convict Two, but Tiffany ran to Nick. She knelt down and pressed her hands against his stomach.

"Get him!" a new voice yelled. "I'll help the human!"

The wolf slunk into the room first, holding its body low to the ground before leaping on Convict Two's back and biting at his neck.

Caitlyn placed the knife into the outstretched hand of Agent Baker. Then she joined Tiffany at Nick's side. Caitlyn winced as she heard the sound of Randy's fangs tearing through delicate flesh. Convict Two howled in pain and frustration. Then he made only guttural sounds until at last he fell silent. When Caitlyn raised her head, Randy had already retreated somewhere. She tried not to look down at the carnage he'd left behind.

"Move." A petite faerie with curly brown hair wearing a black suit like Agent Baker made Caitlyn and Tiffany back away so she could press her hands against his stomach. They began to glow with a faint green light. "He's going to be okay," she said, not to Caitlyn or Tiffany but to Agent Cook, who walked in pushing a makeshift gurney. "We may be able to get away with treating his injury here. Morgan wants to limit outside involvement."

Caitlyn sobbed with relief as Tiffany hugged her.

Agent Cook helped the healer lift Nick onto the gurney. More agents arrived to remove what remained of Convict Two.

"I hope 'Morgan' knows a good dry cleaner," Caitlyn quipped, wiping at her cheeks with the palms of her hands as she surveyed the mess.

Tiffany laughed and hugged her even tighter.

Agent Baker walked over to them and glanced down at the floor. He knelt down to pick up the dagger Caitlyn had dropped. "I thought we took your weapons," Agent Baker said. He carefully pressed against the tip of the blade. She could just make out his eyes widening behind his dark sunglasses as the blade retracted into the handle.

"Relax, B," Caitlyn said. "It's just a prop. Bought it from the gift shop ages ago."

"Cute," he said, returning the dagger to Caitlyn.

"It's my emotional support dagger," she told Tiffany as she slipped it back under the sleeve of her sweater. "Every girl should have one."

"You're amazing," Tiffany said as she gazed at her friend with apparent wonder.

Caitlyn smirked. "I get that a lot."

chapter thirty-nine

Caitlyn walked down a dimly lit hallway on the bottommost floor of Avalon with the most beautiful faerie she'd ever met. "It's not fair how pretty you are," she told Lance. He chuckled.

"You didn't, like, mess with Nick's memories or anything, did you?" Caitlyn asked when they paused outside a door. Lance had needed a special access code and everything.

"No," Lance said. "Anna trusts he understands the importance of discretion. She's good at reading people." He opened the door. "There's a call button when you're ready to leave."

Caitlyn peeked into the room. Nick sat up in a hospital bed, looking at her with an unreadable expression. Everything about the room resembled Amber's room at a real hospital, only the lights gave a faint violet glow instead of the sickly green Caitlyn usually associated with hospitals. And the call button apparently led to something other than a conventional nursing station. She took a deep breath, walked in, and sat in a chair near the bed.

"So, it turns out I was right about the old guy being the Vegas Ripper," Caitlyn told Nick.

"No shit, Sherlock." His eyes lit up with amusement. "I should've known you'd slip out when Tiffany never returned your call."

"How'd you know where to find me, anyway?" Caitlyn asked.

"How did I know world-famous pop star Tiffany Sharp was staying in the executive suite?" Nick asked with a wry grin. "Lucky guess."

"Fair point," Caitlyn said.

"So, do you think he was going after you this time? Or Tiffany?" Nick asked.

"Who knows?" Caitlyn said. "He only ever targeted women when they were alone, but maybe he saw Randy leave and didn't know I was there, or maybe he thought he could take us both. Not like we can ask him now."

"I have to admit I was nervous when I realized you were gone," Nick said. "Then I saw what was happening, and I was terrified."

"It's good that you came," Caitlyn said. "Wish you didn't get hurt, though."

"Yeah." Nick winced. "But did I at least help?"

Caitlyn gave him a soft smile. "You helped."

"I hope you're not just saying that to protect my fragile male ego," Nick said.

"No," Caitlyn said, truthfully. "Anything could have happened in the time it took for Randy and Lance to see what was happening on the security cameras. I may have held off hellhounds with a prop sword, but I don't know how useful a prop dagger would be against the Ripper."

"So, if nothing else, I bought you some time,' Nick said. "I can live with that."

"Next time, you may even stay on your feet!" Caitlyn said.

"Next time?" Nick blanched.

"Sorry," Caitlyn said. "I'm sure life will go back to normal after this."

"Ever since *Dracula*, I find I have to keep redefining 'normal,'" Nick said.

"I understand if..." Caitlyn paused, choking back an unexpected sob. "If you don't want to keep seeing me," she finished.

"Hey," Nick said. "Come here." He held out his arms and Caitlyn carefully curled up beside him. "If things are gonna get weird, well, weirder, there's nobody I'd rather face it with than you." He kissed the top of her head. "I mean, you're pretty handy with weapons, and my kooky survivalist cousin assures me that's the sort of thing you should prioritize in a partner."

Caitlyn laughed.

The ground trembled.

"What the hell was that?" Nick asked.

"Just a little earthquake," Caitlyn said. "Las Vegas is on a fault line, or something. No biggie," she said, but she remained tense. After several minutes passed without any more tremors, Caitlyn closed her eyes and drifted to sleep.

Fortunately, Dan accepted the explanation that the date had gone so well it turned into a two-night affair, but Nick would definitely be back home and ready to return to work—and reality—the following evening.

"Poor guy," Nick told Caitlyn the next morning as she walked with him to the hotel lobby. "That had to sting a little, all things considered. I'm definitely reimbursing him for the tickets no matter what he says." Nick paused and nudged Caitlyn with his shoulder.

Caitlyn broke her gaze from him to look forward. Agent Baker stood off to the side of the lobby with his hands clasped in front of him. He didn't have on his sunglasses. That was a first. He met her eyes but his face remained unreadable. "I'll be right back," she told Nick.

Agent Baker unclasped his hands when Caitlyn approached. She refrained from making any snarky remarks as she accepted his handshake. "It's been a pleasure working with you, Agent B. Where are you going next?"

Agent Baker frowned. "Intel confirms that another outworlder remained on Earth instead of returning home. Convict Five. If you think wolfen are frightening, be thankful you've never seen a reptilian shapeshifter. So many teeth." Agent Baker released an uncharacteristic shudder. "We're pretty sure we know where that one's heading."

"D.C.?"

Agent Baker raised an eyebrow. "Cairo."

"Of course," Caitlyn said. Nothing surprised her anymore. She nearly jumped out of her skin when Nick came up behind her and wrapped an arm around her waist.

"Taking off?" he asked Agent Baker.

Agent Baker nodded. "I don't suppose you can keep this one out of trouble," he said as he slipped on his sunglasses.

"She is the trouble," Nick smoothly replied.

Caitlyn bit her lip on a giggle.

Agent Baker made a weird face, then shook his head as if to clear his brain of whatever intrusive thought entered. He turned to go, but Caitlyn untangled herself from Nick to give him a quick hug. He awkwardly patted her back before clearing his throat.

"See you around, Agent B." Caitlyn let go to give him a mock salute.

chapter forty

I n just a few short weeks, Bianca upended her life in Rochester to start over again in Erie, Pennsylvania. She took a job as a social worker at a homeless shelter affiliated with Kyle's. She also moved into a small two-room apartment with Kyle and his roommate, Ashley Garden, a tiny wisp of a thing with light brown skin, dark brown curls, and a fondness for oversized sweaters and flowing skirts, even in summer. Ashley shared a room with their previous roommate and let Bianca take the bottom bunk. Despite her messy appearance, she kept the room tidy. Like Bianca, she didn't have a lot of things. Her prize possession was an acoustic guitar that occupied one corner.

When Bianca came home from work, Ashley and Kyle sat on a beat-up sofa in the middle of the living room, watching TV with matching horrified expressions.

"Just look at the way she openly flaunts her demonic energy, dancing around with the Deceiver himself." Bianca recognized the angry blond woman as Emerson Fowler's lawyer-turned-girlfriend, Veronica High-more. The feed cut from Veronica and her frosted pink lipstick to a clip of Tiffany Sharp holding a python above her head as she shimmied across the stage in a gold bikini and colorful skirt.

"It's obviously an homage to Britney!" Kyle glared at the screen.

"Bitch," Ashley muttered under her breath.

Bianca stared at the normally soft-spoken Ashley in surprise.

"What?" Ashley said. "I'm not a music snob. I can still appreciate the finely crafted pop songs of my youth," she said as if she was fifty instead of twenty-five.

Bianca chuckled despite her misgivings as the news program cut back to Veronica Highmore. Something about that woman made her skin crawl. She had seen her schtick too many times before, but Veronica's too-perfect appearance in particular sent Bianca straight to the uncanny valley. *It's not just makeup*, she realized.

"Almost time for my gig," Ashley said, rising from the couch.

"You coming?" Kyle asked Bianca.

Bianca shook her head. "Rough day at the office," she said. "I gotta sit this one out."

"The new kid still giving you a hard time?" Kyle gave her an understanding smile.

Bianca pulled a paperback poetry collection out of her bag before she set it down on the coffee table and stretched out on the couch to read after Kyle and Ashley left for the coffee shop. Ashley sang and played guitar one night a week, sometimes two if she went out on open mic night. During the day, she worked at the local library. *It's a shame*, Bianca thought. Ashley had as much natural talent as Tiffany Sharp but none of the otherworldly connections.

Bianca assured herself the negativity she felt had nothing to do with a certain queen of the underworld securing her brother's loyalty.

With a start, Bianca realized she had drifted off to sleep and dropped her book onto the floor. She reached for the cord of an old lamp on the side table to turn on the light. She heard crickets chirping outside. A clock over the television read nine-thirty. Kyle and Ashley would be home soon.

Someone knocked on the door. Bianca stood up and stretched. She tried to look out the peep hole but she had a hard time seeing anything more than a feminine silhouette with the porch light off. Probably their sweet recently-widowed neighbor Millie.

A little late for cookies, Bianca thought as she opened the door.

She gasped.

Now that she saw her in person, Bianca understood why Veronica

Highmore looked so flawless—and so familiar. The family resemblance couldn't be clearer as she looked at the woman's full lips and high cheekbones. Black Anna and Morgan le Fay had an older sister, Bianca remembered. Her real name started with a 'v', too.

Vanessa?

No, Vivienne. That's what they called her.

But why was she accusing Morgan's pet performer of being in league with the devil?

Perhaps more importantly, why was she *here*?

"My dear Emerson is worried you might become a problem for him," Vivienne said. "Again." Her voice somehow sounded both venomous and lovely. "But something tells me you will be more than happy to cooperate with our plan to bring my naughty little sisters to justice." She reached out to caress Bianca's cheek before grasping her chin with a steely grasp.

Bianca couldn't help but turn her head in the direction Vivienne guided her chin. A dark sedan idled in front of the first-floor apartment. Her dismay intensified as the passenger side window lowered to reveal Brian's profile. He turned to look, his face devoid of any emotion or even a hint of recognition.

"What have you done to him?" Bianca asked.

"Come along," Vivienne said without answering. She let go of Bianca's chin to grab her hand and lead her to the car. "I think you and I are about to become good friends."

Bianca had no choice but to follow.

afterword

As I was writing *Devil You Know*, I noticed a lot of parallels with *Drama Queen*. After all, both involve a murder mystery unfolding during preparations for big productions, one in New York City, the other in Las Vegas. Instead of panicking, I leaned into the similarities while using it as an opportunity to play with reader expectations. I also enjoyed seeing events from *Drama Queen* revisited through the eyes of another character who wanted a chance to tell their side of the story.

Bianca and Brian, whose scenes were among my favorite scenes to write in *Girl Next Door*, also returned in *Devil You Know* as the major players moved into position for the world-changing events in next summer's *Dark Angel*.

Oh yeah, it's all coming together now.

'Til next time.

acknowledgments

Thank you to Cari Dubiel, Kaytalin Platt, and G.A. Finocchiaro of Duskbound Books for helping me share my characters and stories with the world.

Thank you to my husband, writer Mike X Welch, for believing in me and my vision.

Thank you to my son Dieter for joining me when I need to touch grass, and to my son Xander for watching anime with me when I want to veg out on the couch instead.

Thank you to my mom, dad, and mother-in-law for your ongoing support and enthusiasm.

Thank you to new and returning readers for taking this journey with me.

Thank you to Lock City Books for your continued support of local writers, and, as always, for rehoming cats with Cat by Cat Inc. faster than my husband can say, "I know you said no more cats, but…"

Thank you to *all* of my little furry friends. Not just my rats, cats, and dog, but the tarantulas I somehow excluded last time. At least I nixed a planned nightmare sequence in *Fallen*. Positive representation only.

about the author

Aly Welch lives in Western New York with her husband, author Mike X Welch, and their twin sons. She has a black belt in modern kenpo karate. Aly also dabbles in acting and aerial gymnastics. She loves exploring the woods, and still hopes to find magic behind every tree and under every rock.

masquerade

A Better Me
Drama Queen
Girl Next Door
Fallen
Devil You Know
Dark Angel (coming 2026)